VENETIAN MAGIC

Jean Morrant

CHIVERS

British Library Cataloguing in Publication Data available

This Large Print edition published by BBC Audiobooks Ltd, Bath, 2009.
Published by arrangement with the Author.

U.K. Softcover   ISBN 978 1 408 442029

Printed and bound in Great Britain by CPI Antony Rowe, Chippenham
and Eastbourne

CHAPTER ONE

Turning swiftly away from yet another dark, inviting gaze, Kate had to admit the busy railway station in Venice was not the best of places for a girl to linger unescorted. Perhaps it had been rather foolish to insist there was absolutely no reason for anyone to meet her, confident she could find her own way to the house. Thank goodness she had taken the trouble to write down the directions her aunt had repeated so patiently.

Moving away from the increasingly persistent young man, she glanced at the instructions which would enable her to complete the journey. Relieved to find the man at the ticket office comprehended her destination, she made her purchase and went towards the pontoon to await the waterbus.

A tremor of excitement rippled through her as she scanned the Grand Canal to the buildings opposite; the tall houses with their peeling façades rising from the water, their shutters closed to the late April sun. Beyond them stood historic buildings crowned by bell towers or shining domes. She was already intrigued by this brief initial glance of Venice and hoped her holiday in this unique city would help erase the dreadful memories of her recent accident and the heartbreak which had

1

followed.

Her excitement mounted as the waterbus pulled away from the landing to chug along the canal amidst boats of varying shapes and sizes until it was time to disembark and make her way towards Campo Lucia. She knew her elderly aunt would be concerned if she failed to arrive in reasonable time, and didn't wish to cause any distress to the lady who had made this exciting visit possible.

Tiring rather quickly in the heat, and wishing she'd chosen to travel in a cool dress rather than the dark blue trousers and jacket she was wearing, she crossed a narrow bridge, pausing on the other side to put down her heavy suitcase. Convinced her aunt's house must be in the immediate vicinity, she spread her map on the stone parapet and was just about to check her position when a foreign voice cut sharply into her thoughts. Having quickly learned to ignore them, she kept her back turned against its owner until a sudden change to perfect English startled her.

'Boy! Are you aware you are trespassing?'

Swinging round to confront her accuser, she removed the baseball cap she'd been wearing, asking sharply, 'Are you speaking to me?'

The tall man advancing towards her appeared quite taken aback, as her hair tumbled around her shoulders, his dark brows lifting in surprise.

'My apologies, signorina, I see I was

2

mistaken. Even so, you are trespassing.'

Her eyes narrowed.

'What made you decide to address me in English?'

'The label on your suitcase,' he pointed out, his voice edged with mockery as he added, 'A common tour company logo, I believe. One could hardly miss it!'

'Then it should have been sufficient to tell you I had merely lost my way and had absolutely no intention of trespassing!' she shot back, infuriated by his manner. 'And now, perhaps you will be kind enough to direct me to Signora Rossini's house. It can't be far from here.'

'Quite so, signorina,' he agreed, stepping forward to take her heavy case. 'In fact, just across the bridge.'

She followed him back over the bridge and round the next corner where he set down her case in the first doorway. Thanking him in her limited Italian, she glimpsed a hint of a smile flickering around his mouth.

'Prego, signorina. In future I suggest you avoid placing yourself in such a vulnerable position. Someone could have led you in the wrong direction, particularly if he was not so unfortunate as to mistake you for a boy.'

Shrugging off the unpleasant thought, she turned back to the heavy wooden door and pressed the bell. A muffled ringing came from within, soon followed by the sound of footsteps when the door opened to reveal a dark-eyed maid.

'Signorina Macleod?' the young woman enquired with a smile, and beckoned Kate into the spacious hallway. 'Please, come in. Signora Rossini is waiting.'

Once inside, it took Kate a moment to adjust to the semi-darkness. Only a faint ray of sunlight penetrated the small, dusty window, revealing the water-marked plaster of bare walls. But the light increased as they ascended the marble steps when Kate looked up to see her Aunt Margaret on the landing, a gentle smile playing on her lips.

'Kathrine! I'm delighted to see you. It's years since you were here!' the signora exclaimed, bestowing kisses on her niece's cheeks as they embraced. 'Come along, you must be exhausted,' she said ushering Kate into a chair. 'Did you have a good journey?'

'Yes, thank you, very straight forward.'

'Good. Rosa will serve tea when she has recovered from the excitement of your arrival. She has been longing to meet my niece from England.'

'On my way here, I was mistaken for a boy by someone you may know.'

'I don't believe it!' Margaret Rossini laughed. 'Who could make a stupid mistake like that?'

'The gentleman who showed me to your door. You see, I took a wrong turning, went

4

over a bridge just round the corner from here when this man very quickly informed me it was private.'

Her aunt nodded.

'That would be Signore Ferrari's man, but I hadn't realised you could speak Italian.'

'I didn't need to, he spoke English!'

Her aunt frowned.

'How strange. Perhaps he guessed who you were and wanted to appear friendly.'

'Quite the reverse, actually,' Kate said with a short laugh. 'In fact, I considered him to be rather arrogant.'

The signora chuckled.

'Never mind, tell me about yourself, Kathrine. Do you enjoy living in London, or do you miss being at home with your parents?'

'Please, call me Kate, everyone else does,' Kate said, then hesitated a moment before she continued. 'Yes, I miss Edinburgh and the family, and since moving south to complete my training I don't have the opportunity to go home quite so often. I expect Mother keeps you informed.'

'Yes, Kate, your mother writes regularly, but it's not quite the same as having one's family close by and you were only a child when I left Scotland.'

'If it hadn't been for my exams I would have come here with mother two years ago, when Uncle Benito died.'

'That was a sad time for me and there are

moments when I feel extremely lonely so I'm pleased to have you here. Beni was a wonderful man,' she declared wistfully then, in an attempt to shake off her sadness, told her, 'You know, I surprised everyone when I allowed a handsome Italian to sweep me off my feet!'

'I can quite understand why. He was very handsome,' Kate commented as she spotted the wedding photograph on the cabinet beside her aunt's chair. 'How old were you then?'

'About your age, my dear, twenty, I believe.'

'I'll be twenty-three on the first of May,' Kate corrected.

'But you look much younger. Now tell me, how do you enjoy being in the nursing profession? And how are you after your accident?'

Kate was reluctant to reveal the unhappy events of the past weeks, but realised her aunt was bound to be curious. Her aunt noticed her reluctance to talk about what had happened.

'I sensed there was more to it than just a slight accident, Kate, but if it's painful to recall . . .'

'No, I've got to face up to it, and no doubt you're wondering why I'm not on duty. Quite frankly, I simply had to get away.'

'You most certainly had! That pretty little face of yours is much too pale and I now realise it has been more serious than I was led to believe.'

'Yes, it was,' she admitted, lowering her eyes, 'that and losing my job, and it's completely over between Greg and me.'

'Oh, my dear, I didn't realise it was anything quite so definite. To lose your private nursing position must have been upsetting for you, and then to lose Greg as well.'

Kate sighed.

'I'll admit I was dreadfully upset at the time, but while I was in hospital I decided against returning to private nursing, and then, on top of that, Greg stopped visiting.'

'Oh, Kate! You must tell me what actually happened, and how badly hurt you were.'

Again Kate hesitated, carefully considering her reply.

'We were driving home after a party,' she began finally. 'The car skidded into a wall and I was knocked unconscious. I had a head injury but it turned out to be less serious than first suspected. You should have seen the sight I was, all the bruising. I'm almost back to normal now.'

'But surely that wasn't the reason Greg neglected you,' her aunt said in astonishment.

Kate shrugged.

'I really don't know. Perhaps he thought I'd be disfigured though, amazingly, I have only one small scar.'

'But it all must have been a dreadful experience for you.'

'I'll admit I was heartbroken at first yet, on

7

reflection, I can't think why. As soon as I began to recover, I realised Greg wasn't the person I thought him to be. I just want to forget him,' Kate said, forcing a bright smile. 'I would like to hear about you, Aunt Margaret, and Venice, of course. From the little I've seen it looks fascinating, and I'm longing to explore.'

'I don't get about as well as I used to,' the signora said as her maid brought in tea. 'However, I'm sure Rosa will take you.'

'I shall be happy to accompany the signorina,' Rosa agreed, giving Kate a shy smile as she set down the tray.

'You will find plenty to occupy your time, and most likely we shall receive an invitation to visit my neighbour, Marco Ferrari, whilst you're here. I believe he's away on business at present but you'll have an opportunity to meet him on his return. He's a charming fellow, and quite influential in the city, wealthy, too. You'll like him,' the signora added quickly.

'What exactly is his business?' she asked, a trifle overawed by the prospect of meeting her aunt's influential neighbour.

'Collecting art is one business he's involved in,' her aunt told her. 'And finance, expert advice, that kind of thing. He's the descendant of a well-known Venetian family whose ancestors were silk merchants, so dealing in financial matters is in his blood. Beni's family were business acquaintances of theirs, and as we are neighbours Marco and I became quite close.'

Kate smiled.

'I'm pleased you have friends nearby. Do you visit each other often?'

'Occasionally. Of course, his home is very grand, much larger than this,' she declared with a sweep of her hand. 'The old, established families had beautiful houses.'

'Sounds quite exciting,' Kate agreed. 'But this house is lovely, too,' she added as her gaze travelled appreciatively round the large salon, a soft sigh escaping her as it came to rest on the high ceiling with its elaborate cornice framing the fading painted scenes.

'In great need of restoration,' her aunt commented wistfully, following her niece's gaze. 'Like many of the old buildings here, the crumbling outer walls betray little of the beautiful interiors, but the upkeep is almost impossible to maintain. Now, I'll take you to your room. Consider this your home for as long as you care to stay.'

'That's very kind of you,' Kate said, following her across the shining terrazzo floors to the large bedroom which had been prepared for her.

'This room's terrific!' she cried, her eyes shining. 'I just know I'm going to like it here.'

'I do hope so,' the signora said, her warm gaze resting thoughtfully on her niece for a moment before she tilted her head to say, 'I believe I hear the telephone so I'll leave you to unpack.'

Once alone with her thoughts, Kate realised how little the memories of Greg had troubled her since her arrival. Also, she was thankful it hadn't been necessary to disclose every detail of the accident, or the reason for her present lack of employment. She uttered a sigh of contentment; at last she could put it all behind her, determined to enjoy what lay ahead.

But her enthusiasm for the coming weeks was quickly dampened when her aunt returned to the room.

'Kathrine, the call is for you.'

'For me?' Kate said, surprised, then laughed. 'Oh, I expect it's my mother making sure I've arrived safely.'

'No, it's a man. He didn't give his name, and I don't recognise the voice.'

Puzzled, Kate went into the hall and picked up the telephone.

'Kathrine Macleod speaking.'

'Kate, it's me, Greg. Glad I've found you.'

'Greg! Why are you ringing me here?' she said crossly. 'I thought we decided to make a clean break.'

'We?' he said with a laugh. 'I think you mean you decided, but I know you didn't mean it.'

'Oh, yes, I did!' she shot back. 'Anyway, how did you know where to find me? I didn't tell you where I was staying.'

'A telephone number is easy enough to find, though there are a few Rossini's in the book.'

'The book?' she echoed. 'You went to the trouble of getting hold of an Italian telephone directory?'

'No problem, Kate, there are plenty of them here, in Venice.'

'You mean you're in Venice right now? Why have you come here?'

'There's something we've got to discuss.'

'I have nothing to discuss with you,' she said and immediately hung up.

CHAPTER TWO

Next morning, Kate flung aside the bed covers to dash across to the balcony overlooking the canal. She watched a boat on its gentle journey, the slow throb of its engines echoing between the high buildings. As it disappeared from sight under a stone bridge it suddenly occurred to her it was the same bridge where she had paused to check her map the previous day only to be accused of trespassing by some arrogant manservant.

The place opposite must be the one her aunt had spoken of, the home of her friend, Signore Ferrari. But the building appeared grim and forbidding, its windows heavily shuttered, and by its outward appearance she couldn't begin to imagine the beautiful interior described to her.

Across the bridge, beyond wrought-iron railings, stood a solid, wooden door set in an arch of grey stone. Nearby, a lower archway reached down to water level, its inlet stoutly guarded by a rusting iron grille. She supposed, being elderly, Signore Ferrari cared little for the outward appearance of his home, his main concern being security during his absence.

'Oh, you're out of bed already! I trust that means you slept well. Not a very exciting view from this side, I'm afraid,' Kate heard and turned to find her aunt had entered the room.

'Come, let's enjoy the hot rolls and coffee Rosa has prepared. I suggest you go shopping with her this morning to help get your bearings, then you can explore to your heart's content.'

After breakfast, finding the weather agreeably warm, Kate chose to wear a sleeveless cotton dress. She hoped to acquire a tan during her stay but gave in to her aunt's suggestion to take her wide-brimmed hat for protection against the midday sun, realising it might also act as a shield against the possibility of being spotted by Greg.

She was worried still as to why he had chosen to come to Venice, and wondered if she had been wise to allow her aunt to believe his phone call had actually come from England. Thankfully, she hadn't been asked to explain the reason she was unemployed, though she felt a trifle guilty over keeping her aunt in ignorance of both these matters. Perhaps it would be better to bring it into the open, when the opportunity arose.

She and Rosa were soon on their way through the busy streets. Eventually, she got her first glimpse of Saint Mark's Square. Ahead stood the Basilica of Saint Mark, its façade a varying mixture of designs, the ancient doorway crowned by glittering mosaics. Rosa smiled at Kate's wondering gaze.

'It's fascinating!' Kate exclaimed breathlessly. 'There's so much to see I can't take it all in at once.'

'Next time we will enter the Basilica,' Rosa promised. 'But now I do the shopping. You will not get lost?'

'Don't worry, I'll return in time for lunch,' Kate assured her laughingly.

Rosa disappeared into the crowd which thronged the narrow street leading away from the piazza, leaving Kate to follow a different route where she feasted her eyes on the sparkling jewellery and pure silk fashions. In another shop a display of glassware made by local craftsmen caught her eye and she paused to admire the treasures within knowing her mother would appreciate such a delicate souvenir. The items looked rather expensive, but maybe there would be something less pricey inside.

Taking off her sun hat, she entered the shop, her tread inaudible on the thick carpet. Carefully picking her way around the huge ornaments displayed, she paused to view a dainty crystal posy bowl on a shelf behind the window display. Then, just as she reached up to see the price ticket, her eye was caught by someone passing outside—someone tall and sandy-haired, very like Greg.

Startled, she gave an involuntary gasp and stepped back from view. But the resounding crash which followed startled her even further when, to her horror, she realised the brim of her hat had caught one of the delicate glass ornaments, sending it crashing on to its marble stand.

At the sight of the shattered object, her eyes widened in shocked dismay. Obviously, this had been one of the more expensive articles on display. The assistant's horrified expression told her as much before he uttered a sound.

'Oh, my goodness, what have I done!' she gasped.

'You have broken it, signorina,' came his stern-faced reply. 'It was,' he continued, with emphasis on the last word, 'one of our best pieces.'

'I'm so sorry. It was an accident. I'm quite prepared to pay for the damage, though I don't consider it entirely my fault. There's hardly room to move in here,' she said with

14

more spirit, but kept her eyes on the window, the brief glimpse of Greg uppermost in her mind.

'The card does say not to touch,' he pointed out.

'Card or no card, it was an accident,' she said heatedly, 'and I have every intention of paying.'

An icy chill ran down her spine when the assistant stated the value of the broken article, and a quick calculation told her the price was out of her reach. She would have to make an arrangement with the bank, assuming she dare venture outside without the risk of encountering Greg.

Glancing nervously from the doorway of the shop, at first she saw no sign of him. But the moment she turned in the direction of home she came face to face with his sneering countenance.

'Causing a bit of a commotion in there, weren't you?' he remarked. 'What was the trouble?'

'Nothing you need concern yourself with,' she replied with forced lightness, 'so there's no point in you hanging around here.'

'But I did telephone,' he said as she made to brush past him. 'Didn't your aunt tell you?'

Not wishing to linger in his company, she asked sharply, 'When?'

'About an hour ago, though I must confess she did her best to dissuade me from seeing you.'

'I only wish she'd succeeded,' she shot back, wishing now she'd had the sense to reveal Greg's arrival in Venice when he telephoned the day before.

'Well, how've you been?' he asked casually.

'How have I been?' she hissed, her cheeks crimson. 'I don't know how you have the nerve to ask! I still have nightmares over that dreadful night. Can't you understand, I don't want to see you ever again.'

'Oh, Kate,' he broke in, 'I know I've been a cad, and I realised my mistake as soon as I found you'd left. I was so desperate to see you I got the first plane out of London, and I want to make it up to you, if you'll allow me.'

'No, Greg, it's no use. We have already agreed not to see each other again,' she said as coolly as she could manage.

'No, as I reminded you yesterday, it was you who decided.'

'Whoever it was, I didn't expect to see you here, and I'd prefer it if you don't phone again. I mean it, Greg, just keep out of my life!'

'Whether you like it or not, I'm staying,' he said with a derisive curl of his lip. 'There's a bit of business I must discuss with you.'

'I don't want to hear it, Greg. In fact, should we chance to meet again, I shall ignore you completely.'

'Not after you've heard what I have to say,' he began, but Kate had already started to

16

hurry away.

Disturbed by her encounter with Greg, she rushed back to the house, to find her aunt standing by the telephone. Her heart sank. Did it mean Greg had rung again?

'Ah, Kate, here you are! I've got some quite exciting news.'

'Aunt Margaret, before you say any more I'd like to apologise. Yesterday, I chose not to mention Greg was in Venice as there was no point in worrying you unnecessarily, but I now know he has telephoned again.'

'Yes, dear, just after you left this morning.'

'I'm really sorry about that, but he won't trouble you further as I've told him I want no more contact.'

'Very wise, just what he deserves,' the older woman declared. 'But it is Marco's call I want to tell you about. He rang just a few moments ago to invite us to a dinner party he is giving this evening. I was sure you'd be pleased as it will give you an opportunity to see inside the palazzo.'

'Oh, yes, great!' Kate responded, relieved to know it hadn't been Greg pestering her again. 'But I thought you said he was away.'

'Had to return early, something to do with the security of the art exhibition he's planned. I'm not sure of the details. He's been away buying pictures, you see, so I expect it's connected with that.'

'Oh, I see. Well, I've been looking forward

to meeting him, and I hope you can advise me about what I should wear.'

'I notice you've brought one or two very pretty dresses, so choose the most feminine as I suspect he's not in favour of the modern trend in fashion which some young people are wearing here.'

'Never worry, I won't let you down.'

'Apart from meeting that awful Greg fellow, did you enjoy your morning?' the signora enquired as they went into the sitting-room.

'Yes, I had a good look round the piazza,' she replied, relieved her aunt didn't pursue the subject of Greg.

'If Marco takes a liking to you he may offer to accompany you to places of particular interest.'

'I don't suppose he'll want to act as tour guide,' Kate replied, 'particularly to someone of my age.'

'Why not? He's very proud of Venice, and I can't see that age matters.'

'But he may not be so keen to offer if he hears of my fiasco this morning,' Kate put in, and went on to relate what had happened in the glass shop. 'Of course, I intend to pay for the damage.'

After taking the short rest her aunt prescribed, Kate decided on her dress for the evening. She laid it on the bed in readiness and, hopeful of adding a little height to her own five feet two, selected matching high-heeled sandals. There was time to spare before she changed and, anxious to gain a little more knowledge of the Italian language in preparation for the coming evening, she sought Rosa's help. But Rosa was too excited about the impending visit and held Kate's dress against her admiringly.

'Tonight you will meet Signore Ferrari and see the beautiful rooms and paintings. I am so happy for you.'

'I'm quite looking forward to meeting him,' Kate agreed. 'By what my aunt says, he sounds a very nice person.'

'Oh, yes, he is, and I am pleased he has returned, though I hope the signora did not come with him,' Rosa said, laying Kate's dress on the bed.

'I didn't realise he was married.'

'No, they are not married. He employs her for the art,' Rosa declared, yet her lip curled as she added, 'But she wishes to be his wife, I can tell!'

'But maybe Signore Ferrari likes her,' Kate tried to reason. 'People of his age often marry purely for companionship, you know.'

Rosa's only reply came in the form of a derisive snort as she swept from the room.

After taking a shower, Kate slipped into the blue dress, smoothing the silky material over her slender waist. At the dressing table, she applied a hint of eye shadow above her wide grey eyes, and flicked her hair forward to frame her face. She found her aunt, awaiting her in the main salon, looking splendid in black, her silvery hair coiled softly on to the crown of her head.

'You look lovely, my dear,' she complimented Kate as they left the apartment. 'Blue suits you.'

'Being invited to a palace is exciting,' Kate whispered, shaking off her feelings of anxiety as they crossed the narrow, stone bridge, 'but how shall I address him? Does he have a special title, or do I simply say signore?'

'Good gracious, no, he wouldn't expect it,' her aunt assured. 'Just be your normal self, nothing more.'

This evening, the huge, wooden doors set in the high, stone wall stood open with the unexpected delight of a fountain playing gently into a garden pool before them, sheltered by a magnolia tree, its wax-like flowers already in bloom. Kate could hardly believe the dismal wall would enclose such a pretty courtyard.

'Come along or we shall be late,' the signora urged as she led the way towards the impressive marble steps. 'Most of the guests will arrive by boat. I noticed one or two moored by the bridge, but it is difficult to reach the front entrance now the steps are partially submerged, particularly earlier in the year.'

'Is it true the sinking may be arrested?' Kate queried.

'Possibly. As I understand, a great number of architects and engineers have been involved in making plans to prevent it,' the signora informed her as they passed between tall glass doors.

Kate paused on the threshold of the magnificent room, allowing her gaze to travel up to the two immense crystal chandeliers which hung from a ceiling filled with beautiful frescoes in delicate colours.

'It's beautiful,' she whispered. 'I never dreamed of anything like this!'

She crossed to the balcony, leaning over the stone parapet to view the busy Grand Canal. Truly a palace, she thought, spotting the blue and gilt mooring posts by the partly submerged steps leading to the imposing entrance below.

Kate turned as the sound of voices drifted out from the main salon where guests assembled to sip an aperitif. She was convinced her limited knowledge of their language and culture would cause her to feel an outsider. However, just as she prepared to join them, a voice which she immediately recognised sounded close behind.

'Ah, Signora Rossini, I have been searching for you!'

The signora drew Kate to her side.

'Just arrived, Marco,' she said, 'but first let me introduce you. Signore Ferrari, this is Kathrine Macleod, my niece.'

Speechless, Kate looked up to meet the

man's smiling blue eyes when, barely able to conceal her embarrassment, she managed to utter a formal greeting.

'Let us dispense with formalities, Kathrine,' he suggested as his outstretched hand found hers to grip it warmly. 'My name is Marco, and I welcome you to my home.'

Kate had compressed her lips in case they should have fallen apart in surprise, and in a daze she heard him say to her aunt, 'So this is the young lady of whom you have spoken. This becomes our second meeting,' he continued with a twinkle in his eyes, 'although I had absolutely no idea who you were on first acquaintance.'

'You've already met?' Kate's aunt intervened, casting Kate a faintly reproachful glance.

'Yes, but I didn't realise it at the time,' Kate admitted, her cheeks growing warm under his mocking gaze. 'Naturally, I presumed . . .'

'The fault was entirely mine,' he offered quickly. 'Come, let me get you an aperitif.'

Kate listened while he discussed his plans for the next exhibition, emphasising his words by gestures of his well-shaped hands. Undoubtedly, he was the most handsome man in the room, tall and dark, and wearing a white dinner jacket with the true bearing of a cultured man. How could she have mistaken him for a manservant!

He turned to catch her stare, the shadows

from the wall lights accentuating his high cheekbones, and his gaze stayed teasingly upon her as she sipped her drink, until someone caught his attention.

'Ah! I see the last of my guests have arrived,' he said, inclining his head slightly as he moved away.

As he crossed the room her aunt drew closer.

'So it was Marco you spoke to on the day you arrived?' she said.

'Yes, I'm sure he thought I'd lost my way on purpose, and he had the cheek to lecture me!'

'At the time he wasn't to know who you were,' her aunt pointed out, 'but now you appear to be giving a good impression.'

'For your sake, I'm pleased, but he shouldn't presume,' she objected. 'Now I suspect he's laughing at me.'

'Nonsense!' the signora exclaimed. 'He's a true Venetian gentleman.'

Kate sighed. Perhaps she had been over-sensitive. She shouldn't have allowed herself to be provoked by his previous manner. She sighed thoughtfully yet, as he advanced towards them, she couldn't help but admire his good looks and grace, and as his hand rested lightly beneath her elbow, she experienced an unaccountable sensation of pleasure.

'Come, meet everyone before we dine,' he said, urging her towards one of the most strikingly elegant women Kate had ever seen, whose crimson lips parted in a smile as they drew near. But the smile never reached her eyes, and very soon Kate was meeting that cold, dark stare.

'Camilla,' Marco was saying, 'I would like you to meet Signora Rossini's niece, Miss Kathrine Macleod. Kathrine, this is a friend, Signora Verdi.'

'Ah, so you are the young lady from England,' Signora Verdi drawled in heavily-accented English, her bejewelled hand touching Kate's only briefly. 'I hope you are enjoying a taste of Venetian culture and trust you have not felt too ill at ease.'

'Camilla!' he reproached softly. 'I hope you are not suggesting . . .'

She turned to him with an expression of innocence.

'No, caro, merely sympathetic. It must be quite daunting for Miss Macleod to adjust to our ways and language so soon after her arrival.'

Kate bit back the first retort which came to mind and replied stiffly, 'To the contrary, I find it most relaxing.'

Shooting her a cool, disinterested glance, the signora turned to Marco with an endearing smile and reverted to their familiar tongue.

Returning the conversation to English, Marco asked, 'Where is this art expert you brought with you, Camilla? Kathrine may like to meet him.'

With a bored expression, Camilla turned away, raising her hand to draw someone forward.

'Signore Jonathan Webb from New York,' she said as the man disengaged himself from the centre of the group nearby. 'Jonathan, meet Miss Kathrine Macleod.'

Puzzled, Kate met the narrowed gaze of the man who came to a sudden halt before her.

'I believe we've already met,' she started to say, searching her memory for where she had encountered him before.

'You already know each other?' Marco asked in surprise.

Before she had the chance to respond, Jonathan Webb merely raised his dark brows to reply without interest, 'No, I have not met this lady.'

CHAPTER THREE

Feeling somewhat foolish, Kate watched as Jonathan Webb moved away, soon lost from view in the crowded room.

'I must have been mistaken,' she said, though still convinced she had met this man somewhere before, even if his manner had been cool.

'It may be someone your aunt has mentioned,' Marco suggested. 'She knows so many people here. Quite a number of the gentlemen present are business acquaintances,' he continued as they went towards the dining-room, 'but tonight I shall mix business with pleasure. When Signora Rossini spoke of your visit it was my wish she should bring you here. Little did I realise we would meet on the day of your arrival, so already I feel we are quite well acquainted.'

'It was kind of you to invite me,' she murmured, attempting to give him her full attention, although still puzzled over the American. 'I'm pleased to have the opportunity to see inside such a splendid house.'

'The pleasure is mine, signorina,' he said, adding with a hint of a smile, 'And never again will I mistake you for a boy.'

Kate felt extremely aware of his masculine presence as he held her chair, seating her between himself and the elderly businessman who had been chatting to her aunt. She couldn't fail to notice the admiring glance he bestowed upon her as he took his seat. Recalling the moment they'd first met with sudden humour she smiled, unfolding her napkin.

'What is it that makes you smile, Kathrine?' he queried softly, pronouncing her name in such an attractive way she lost the desire to ask him to shorten it.

'I was remembering the first time we met,'

26

she disclosed, 'when I inadvertently trespassed on your property.'

He lowered a dark brow, simulating disapproval.

'And you assumed me to be a manservant at the palazzo.'

'I believe we both assumed,' she countered, seeing the light of amusement in his eyes, 'though, naturally, as a friend of Signora Rossini I imagined you to be a much older person.'

'Ah, but in this country men of all ages treasure the beautiful things in life,' he rejoined with a roguish smile, 'and a pretty face is one of them.'

Kate felt extremely vulnerable under his gaze, and was relieved when the gentleman seated on her other side engaged her in conversation. Then, as the next course was being served, Marco caught her attention again.

'As you are new to Venice, perhaps you will allow me to escort you through the city and reveal to you its many treasures. Providing Signora Rossini approves, of course.'

'Thank you, signore, I'm sure she will.'

'Marco, please,' he reminded her, and went on to say, 'I think it better you do not go alone. The tourist season is upon us when an unsuspecting young lady may fall into the trap of the shrewd, and sometimes unscrupulous, Venetian.'

'Really?' she said, her eyes widening. 'I wouldn't have thought it was that kind of place.'

Chuckling at her expression of disbelief, he nodded.

'Oh, yes, believe me, the torment of money unspent—palms itch at the very thought of it!'

'Now you're teasing me,' she reproached with a smile.

"I must also protect you from the Romeos,' he continued. 'My countrymen do not always take "no" for an answer.'

'You've no need to worry about me, Marco. I'm quite old enough to take care of myself.'

He smiled.

'I doubt your age will save you from the pitfalls I have mentioned. Venice is a city steeped in romance from which very few visitors escape, and once the magic has worked its spell even you, mia caro, will not be immune!'

'I came for a rest and to see the treasures you spoke of, not in search of romance,' she declared firmly, finding his manner faintly irritating.

In reply, he raised the sparkling crystal glass he held.

'To your holiday,' he said, smiling, 'and may you not be disappointed.'

There had been no sign of Jonathan Webb at dinner, nor was he anywhere in sight when they gathered for coffee and liqueurs in the salon. Kate had felt curiously uneasy as she puzzled over the American, and it was only when her aunt mentioned Marco's forthcoming art exhibition that her mind was jolted by a sudden recollection of where she had met him before. It had been in a London gallery when Greg had introduced her to members of the art world. Jonathan Webb had been amongst them.

She remembered him now, the rather arrogant, self-proclaimed expert of the group, but she didn't recall him having the accent of an American. It seemed odd that someone Greg had once introduced to her should also be in Venice, and pretending he had never met her previously.

As Kate drank her coffee she saw Camilla take a possessive hold on Marco's arm. But as he circulated amongst his guests she noticed him gently disengage her hand from his sleeve before coming to a halt at her aunt's side.

'Camilla forgets I have other guests,' he apologised, and went on to say, 'I suggested to Kathrine it may be helpful if I were to accompany her on her explorations. You know how difficult it can be for anyone alone.'

Signora Rossini nodded.

'Very wise, Marco,' she agreed. 'I shall know she is in good hands.'

'Then I am at your disposal, Kathrine,' he said, just as Camilla came to a halt beside them. 'Perhaps you will let me know a convenient time.'

'Do not forget your exhibition, caro,' Camilla reminded him. 'It will not leave you much free time. I am sure Miss Macleod will be quite safe. Most tourists manage perfectly well without a personal guide.'

Kate caught Marco's frown of disapproval before her aunt intervened.

'One can hardly describe my niece as a tourist. She's staying at least a month, maybe longer.'

'Then we have plenty of time,' Marco said, 'and your aunt will feel more at ease if you allow me to escort you.'

'Thank you, but I don't want to take up your time when you have an exhibition to arrange,' Kate said uncomfortably.

With a casual shrug Marco turned away leaving Kate to wonder if she should accept his invitation, or was he a typical Latin of the kind he himself had warned her against?

Kate spent many disturbed hours throughout the night, troubled by Greg's appearance in Venice, and the chance meeting of Webb, someone curiously forgetful of their past introduction. She wondered, was it merely a coincidence, or was there a connection between the two men which brought them both to Venice at the same time? And what possible reason would Webb have for pretending they were total strangers?

When morning came at last, she

remembered she had to call in at the glass shop, hoping this time there would be no Greg in the vicinity. Relieved to see no sign of him as she made her way to the shop, she made a careful entrance, nervously avoiding the delightful but delicate wares on display.

'I promised to come back,' she began brightly when she spotted the assistant, 'although I don't intend to cause any trouble today.'

Her voice faltered to nothing as a tall figure she immediately recognised emerged from the rear of the shop.

'You don't intend to cause trouble, signorina?' Marco queried. 'Is there a problem of some kind between you and Luigi?'

She uttered a sigh of annoyance when she realised he appeared to be awaiting an explanation for the reason for her visit. But it was the assistant who spoke first in rapid Italian and Marco's firm lips quirked with amusement as Luigi gestured to the spot where the broken ornament had fallen.

'I assume he has told you his version of what happened yesterday,' she began with a cool glance in the assistant's direction, 'and I hope he mentioned that I have already offered to pay.'

'I understand from Luigi it was merely an unfortunate accident, so I beg you not to distress yourself further,' he assured kindly.

'But I must explain to the proprietor,' she

insisted, opening her bag to gather the few notes from within. 'I don't have sufficient money on me, so if I leave my name and address, will you be kind enough to vouch for me?'

His hand covered her own briefly.

'Please, close your purse. I will explain to the proprietor.'

Then, after speaking briefly to Luigi, he took her arm.

'Let me escort you back, otherwise you may get lost again.'

Grateful for his presence in case Greg should pass her way, she stayed beside him as they left the shop, but once outside in the narrow street she came to a halt.

'I don't wish to give the impression I'm using my aunt's friendship with you as a reason for not paying,' she declared firmly. 'I would have preferred to speak to the proprietor myself.'

'It is not necessary, Kathrine,' he said, a hint of laughter in his voice. 'Signora Rossini will explain.'

The following morning, Kate was out shopping with Rosa when Marco telephoned. On her return she learned her aunt had accepted an invitation from him on her behalf, to act as Kate's guide.

'Oh, no, I'm sure he was only being polite,' she declined, still piqued by Camilla's remarks.

Signora Rossini flung down her newspaper.

'I think I know Marco well enough to decide whether or not he was being polite!' she said exasperatedly. 'He has an unlimited knowledge of Venice's history which is exactly what you wanted, isn't it?'

Kate hesitated uncomfortably.

'I know, but must it be today?'

'Last night you accepted so, naturally, I assumed you'd be eager to go. I trust you haven't allowed Camilla to discourage you.'

'She gave me the impression he was merely being polite and I sensed she thought I was trying to ingratiate myself with him.'

'You shouldn't listen to anything she says. She behaves like a spoiled child. Even widowhood hasn't matured her and she continues to have tantrums if she doesn't get her own way,' her aunt disclosed. 'Between ourselves, Marco tolerates a great deal because of his close friendship with her late husband, Carlo, who was a brilliant artist. Carlo was an orphan, and it was Marco's parents who took him in and paid for his education, including his years at the art college. He and Marco grew up together, almost like brothers.'

'I see,' Kate said, curiously relieved. 'That explains a lot. I must try to be more sympathetic.'

A thoughtful, little smile played round the signora's mouth.

'Quite frankly, I suspect Camilla is not the

broken-hearted widow she professes to be,' she said with an expressive lift of her shoulders. 'But, there again, it is none of my business.'

Kate couldn't account for her unexpected feeling of elation when Marco arrived. She was just adding the final touches to her make-up when she caught the sound of his voice drifting from the salon.

'I have brought the launch round to the bridge,' he was saying. 'Perhaps a tour of the Canal Grande would be a good way to start, yes?'

'Everywhere is new to Kate,' her aunt was enthusing. 'She was thrilled when I told her of your invitation.'

Kate smiled to herself, and when she entered the salon to see Marco standing by the open window, the sting of Camilla's tongue ceased to trouble her. His casual, but immaculate attire suited him well. A fine black sweater above well-cut grey slacks added a look of lithe grace to his muscular form.

'You are ready to leave, Kathrine?' he asked as his gaze lingered on her appreciatively.

'Please, call me Kate.'

'I prefer to call you Kathrine,' he said, repeating her name in his sensual Latin voice.

Her heart seemed to skip a beat but she managed a croaky little, 'If you wish,' and allowed her hand to rest in his as they descended the stairs.

34

Out in the brilliant sunshine, they made their way to where his launch was moored.

'Today, I grant you the freedom of my bridge!'

He laughed, bringing a smile to her face.

'From this point we will take a gentle cruise along the Grand Canal, then I suggest we call at a little café in a quiet backwater where you can tell me all about yourself, and the reason behind your sudden decision to visit Venice.'

Kate shot him an anxious glance as he helped her into the launch, wondering how much he already knew, or could it be merely friendly curiosity on his part?

'I'd prefer to talk about Venice,' she said, releasing his hand. 'I understand you're an authority on the subject.'

'Just as you wish,' he conceded. 'I shall enjoy having your company whatever topic of conversation we choose.'

After making sure she was comfortably seated, he started the engine and cast off, pulling smoothly away in the direction of the wide canal.

'This is wonderful,' she breathed as she relaxed to take in the view. 'I didn't expect to do my sightseeing by private launch.'

'Bene! Enjoy yourself,' he said, raising a hand. 'Here is the Rialto Bridge, and the Ca da Mosto, thirteen century, much older than my home.'

'But your home is beautiful, Marco,' she

enthused. 'Well, the part I saw.'

'Then you must come again, to see the rest of the palazzo. Perhaps dinner one evening, but this time without my business acquaintances.'

'But the signora, she may object. I mean . . .' she began, then turned away to hide her confusion as a gleam of amusement sparkled in his eyes.

'Do you mean Camilla?' he queried, his free hand turning her to face him. 'Why do you mention her?'

'Well, I understand your exhibition will be held quite soon. She may need to discuss it with you.'

'You must not regard her too seriously,' he advised. 'She's inclined to be a little outspoken at times, though quite competent when it comes to organising an exhibition.'

Furious with herself for mentioning Signora Verdi, Kate asked casually, 'And the American she introduced to me, Jonathan Webb I believe was his name, will he be employed to advise on the display?'

'I haven't employed him. That is for Camilla to decide. According to her, he had seen the exhibition advertised and volunteered his assistance.'

'Oh, I see,' she said quietly and returned her attention to the buildings.

Marco continued in his rôle of guide as they cruised along between the slender gondolas, water buses, and water taxis, each ploughing their way along the street of sun-dappled water. Eventually, he steered the launch into the maze of narrow backwaters, slowing the engine to a soft purr as the sounds from the busy canal faded. Expertly manipulating the controls, he pulled in at a mooring beside a short flight of worn, stone steps. Kate watched whilst he secured the boat until, aware of his gaze, she glanced away to follow the silent glide of a passing gondola.

'Would you like to ride in a gondola?' he asked pleasantly, breaking the uneasy silence which had fallen between them.

'Oh, yes,' she replied with a spark of enthusiasm. 'They're so elegant, and very kind of, well . . .'

'Romantic,' he supplied. 'Could that be the word you search for?'

'Mm, I suppose it is.'

Marco chuckled.

'And have you come to Venice in search of romance?' he asked, his blue eyes meeting hers as he lifted one foot on to the steps. 'Will you allow the magic of Venice to capture your heart?'

'I believe I told you once before, romance is the last thing I have in mind,' she declared lightly, even though she found his close scrutiny rather disturbing.

Marco merely smiled and reached down, about to take her hand when, quite unexpectedly, a boat shot round the corner just ahead of them, the roar of its powerful engine echoing between the tall buildings. There was a bump, and a spray of water hit Kate as she lost her balance, falling heavily against the side of the boat.

In seconds Marco had jumped down beside her, helping her back on to the seat, his expression one of deep concern as he asked, 'Are you hurt?'

For a few moments she was speechless and remained in the supporting curve of his arm. When eventually she managed to shake her head, he let out a sigh of relief.

'Take it easy,' he advised quickly. 'I'll fetch a blanket from the locker otherwise you will soon feel cold. I wish I'd seen the crazy fool who did this. I would report him to the authorities!'

'Please, Marco, don't worry, I'll be all right when I get my breath back,' she managed to gasp. 'Accidents will happen.'

'This was no accident,' he exclaimed. 'It was extremely irresponsible behaviour! There are speed regulations on the canals, and for safety's sake they should be adhered to.'

By now, a small group had gathered at the water's edge, all wide-eyed with interest, their voices increasing in pitch.

'Signore!' one called. 'You need an ambulance for your loved one?'

'No, no, grazie, but maybe a little brandy

will help,' Marco suggested when the proprietor of a nearby café rushed to the scene.

'Ah, Signore Ferrari!' the man exclaimed, his hands raised in a dramatic gesture. 'Two large brandies, immediately!' he cried, dashing off to attend to Marco's wishes.

'Did you witness the incident?' Marco asked the group of onlookers. 'Maybe one of you recognised the boat, or who was at the helm?'

They looked at each other and shrugged, then one man volunteered, 'No, signore, just the gold flash along its bows, rather like the form of a bird, nothing more.'

Kate felt Marco tense.

'Grazie. You have a keen eye, signore,' he said. 'I was too concerned for my passenger to notice, but I intend to find the idiot responsible!'

CHAPTER FOUR

'Signore, to help restore your strength,' said the café proprietor as he placed a tray on the steps and with a nod of acknowledgement, Marco pressed a glass into Kate's hand.

'Try this. You'll feel much better.'

Kate found the amber liquid warming and soon her trembling had almost ceased. But she noticed the lines of tension were still visible in

Marco's expression as he spoke sharply into his mobile phone before returning to his position at the wheel.

'I shall take you back to the palazzo,' he decided, starting the engine once more and turning the boat on the narrow canal. 'You must get out of those wet clothes.'

'They are a little uncomfortable,' she admitted with a rueful smile, 'but I'll be fine after I've dried off.'

Alongside the palazzo's private mooring, Marco secured the launch and lifted her from it, disregarding his own discomfort as he negotiated the partly-submerged, slippery steps.

'I deeply regret this happening,' he said as he set her on her feet.

Still in the circle of his arm, Kate looked up, smiling.

'I'll just think of it as a sort of initiation ceremony,' she began to say, but then she saw his eyes darken and he drew her closer, holding her gaze as his lips came down to capture hers.

The unexpected kiss startled her, brief as it was.

'Kathrine,' he murmured. 'I find you so very tempting.'

Inside the palazzo, Marco gave instructions for his housekeeper to take Kate to one of the large dressing-rooms where she could change into a thick towelling robe while her dress was dried and pressed.

'But I could go home and change,' she protested. 'I don't want to give your staff extra work.'

'It is no trouble, really,' he insisted, 'and, as you are here, you may like to continue your tour of Venice in my library. A quiet rest would be advisable as I'm sure you must be feeling rather shaken after your experience. We can take out the launch another day, that is, if you won't feel too nervous.'

She smiled.

'I'm sure I won't. It will be something to look forward to.'

He glanced down at his sodden footwear.

'I also must change,' he said with a rueful smile. 'See you in the library in about twenty minutes.'

In the well-appointed dressing-room, Kate took off her damp dress and handed it over to the housekeeper, and after washing the canal water from her hair in the adjoining bathroom she dried her wet hair, her thoughts dwelling on Marco.

During the short time they had spent together, he had been an informative and entertaining guide but, after the incident on the canal, she had noticed his expression become strained, and his manner towards her became almost protective. But was it that same protective instinct which had prompted him to kiss her? Kate thought not, yet the touch of his

41

lips lingered in her thoughts as she wrapped the towelling robe around her and prepared to join him in the library downstairs.

Marco had already selected a number of books which were on the reading table. Some illustrated Venetian art and others had details of the city's architecture, all of which Kate found so interesting time passed almost unnoticed.

'You will dine with me?' Marco invited when she remarked on the hour.

She glanced down at the robe she was wearing and said with a smile, 'I'm hardly dressed for dinner.'

Marco grinned.

'Don't worry, I shall enjoy having a meal without any traces of formality.'

'Then I will go and change into my very informal gown,' she told him and returned to the dressing-room to find her dress already waiting.

During dinner, he described the places she had yet to visit and her enthusiasm for the unique city increased throughout the meal. But as they sipped coffee from dainty, gold-rimmed cups she sensed the conversation was drifting towards the reason she was in Venice, and she broke in.

'My aunt was right, you're quite an authority on Venetian architecture.'

He gave a modest shrug.

'I'm pleased the day has ended a little better

42

than anticipated after the accident on the canal.'

'Accident or incident?' she queried. 'Surely no-one would have done that on purpose.'

'Perhaps you are right,' he agreed quickly, though not too convincingly she thought, 'and as you didn't suffer any serious consequences, I think it better we forget it ever happened.'

She nodded, though was secretly surprised that he should now brush aside a matter which had made him so angry at the time. Glancing at her watch, she gave a reluctant sigh and got to her feet.

'I had no idea it was so late.'

'I'm sure the signora will guess where you are,' he assured her, rising from the table, and then his expression turned a little anxious when he suggested, 'Perhaps it would be advisable not to mention the accident. It may upset her.'

As she left the palazzo by way of the garden where the sweet scent of flowers hung on the still evening air, he paused to look down on her, his eyes glittering in the faint light.

'Were you shocked by what happened earlier?' he asked softly.

'You mean on the boat?'

He chuckled.

'No, no, I was referring to the moment when I kissed you.'

'No, Marco, not shocked, just a bit startled.'

'You looked so helpless, so tempting.'

'And wet,' she put in with a wry smile.

'Kathrine,' he whispered softly and kissed her again.

Kate closed her eyes as his arm tightened about her, her heartbeats quickening at the pleasurable sensation of his warm lips on her own.

'Yes, so very tempting, mia caro,' he whispered as he drew away from her. 'May I call you tomorrow?'

'I'll look forward to that,' she responded happily.

He brushed her cheek with his fingers as he drew open the heavy door.

Later, as she undressed, she recalled this moment with Marco and asked herself why a mere kiss should have put her mind in such turmoil. Dare she allow that magic moment to be repeated, or would it only take her headlong into further heartbreak?

The following day Marco telephoned whilst Kate was writing a letter home and she heard her aunt invite him to lunch.

'You see, it is Kate's birthday,' the signora continued, and by her smiling responses, Kate guessed he had accepted.

She uttered a contented sigh. The morning post had brought numerous cards, including a cheque from her parents, and her aunt had given her perfume. But the most unexpected gift was from Rosa who had shyly thrust a parcel into her hands. On opening it, Kate had been delighted to find a small blue crocheted bag of unusual design, the top drawn together by a thin, gilt chain.

To her relief there was no word from Greg, so it seemed their last conversation had deterred him from attempting to contact her further.

Marco arrived promptly at one, dressed more formally than on the previous day, and as he strode across the salon to greet her, she silently admired the light suit he was wearing.

'May I wish you a very happy birthday, Kathrine,' he said, handing her a single red rose, its long stem encased in ribbon and silver foil.

Delighted by the romantic gesture, Kate thanked him and breathed in the sweet fragrance from the perfect bloom.

As they were served a dry, sparkling wine to celebrate the occasion, Marco glanced at the cards and gifts on the table beside him.

'You haven't been forgotten,' he remarked. 'Someone must miss you.'

'Yes, I expect my parents do, although I'm not sure I won't want to leave here when the time comes,' she confessed with a sigh.

'No-one else?' he said softly, regarding her with a question in his eyes.

'No, no-one,' she confirmed on a faintly bitter note.

'Then let us make the most of your time here,' he suggested. 'Perhaps you would enjoy riding in a gondola later this evening. Venice is spectacular after dark.'

Kate experienced a glow of pleasure at this suggestion but noticed he seemed to avoid any conversation concerning the previous day. She wondered about those moments in his arms, and the kisses they'd shared. Had it been merely a gesture for which he held little regard? She had found his kiss curiously exciting and, on reflection, Greg had never caused her heart to pound in anticipation of the next embrace.

After coffee was served, Rosa announced a call for Marco. With a sigh of exasperation, he went to the telephone where his conversation was brief, his tone impatient, and Kate observed his taut expression when he returned to the table.

'It is most unfortunate, but something has occurred which calls for my attention. I hope you will excuse me, signora.' Turning to Kate, he said, 'Do forgive me. I hope this will not delay our outing.'

'Of course. It will be something to look forward to, whenever you're free.'

'Marco appeared quite angry,' Kate remarked to her aunt once they were alone. 'I wonder what's wrong?'

'I expect Camilla is having one of her tantrums. By what I could gather from his conversation, it seems she wants a plan of the palazzo immediately so that the display of pictures can be decided upon. As if it couldn't have waited until lunch was over,' Aunt Margaret sighed. 'Poor Marco, he never has a moment's peace.'

'Perhaps all this attention to paintings reminds her of the past, particularly if some of them were painted by her husband,' Kate remarked. 'She may still be upset over his death.'

'Upset? Pah!' the signora brushed the suggestion aside. 'No, Camilla's not in the least sentimental about Carlo's work. She now thrives on having a string of admirers, particularly those who are wealthy.'

'And is Marco one of them?' Kate found the courage to ask, her sympathy for Camilla decreasing.

'Marco has a strong sense of duty, but he's too shrewd, even for Camilla's clever wiles, to be swayed by beauty alone,' with a surreptitious smile the signora added, 'Do remember, it was to you he gave the rose.'

'What on earth has a rose got to do with it?'

'An old Venetian custom, my dear. When a man gives a girl a single red rose on the first of May it is because he wishes to further their acquaintance.'

'Surely you don't think Marco . . .' Kate stammered.

'I most certainly do!' Aunt Margaret interrupted with a chuckle. 'He's not the kind of man who makes frivolous gestures.'

Kate shook her head.

'It's a charming custom, I agree,' she said then, in an attempt to quell the surge of happiness within her, added, 'but I don't want to get too involved with anyone.'

'Given time, your bitterness will subside, you'll see,' came the wise response. 'I suspect you already like Marco more than you care to admit.'

'Even so, I wouldn't risk placing my aspirations on an old Venetian custom,' she said, and to avoid the older woman's keen gaze Kate crossed to the window overlooking the canal.

By the narrow bridge she noticed a launch was moored with a dark-haired man lounging at the wheel, idly smoking a cigar. She assumed the launch had brought Camilla to the palazzo, and let her gaze travel the length of the boat. But when she caught sight of the bold insignia on the bows, she drew a sharp breath, recalling the observations of the man who witnessed the accident on the canal the day before. She was looking at an emblem in the shape of a golden hawk, and he had likened the one on the offending boat to that of a large bird!

Kate's first thoughts were to bring it to Marco's attention, then checked herself. Half of all the craft in Venice could be displaying such an emblem, and this just happened to be Camilla's. With a wavering sigh she returned to her chair, her mind on the raven-haired beauty. She wondered, had Marco presented the rose in the hope of furthering their acquaintance, or was he, a mature and more experienced man, merely flattered by her attention?

However, that evening, when he telephoned to ask if she was still willing to take the promised gondola ride, she couldn't suppress the delight which rose within her and accepted without hesitation.

Barely twenty minutes later, Kate opened the door to her smiling escort, immaculate in his dark suit as he walked beside her to the water's edge where a waiting gondola gently buffeted against its moorings. With the aid of Marco and the straw-hatted gondolier, she boarded the shining black craft with its flower-filled vases and sank into the velvet cushions. Once Marco was seated beside her, the gondolier took up his position, grasping the long pole to pilot his craft.

It was quiet on the canal, with only the warning cry of a passing boatman or a distant peal of laughter breaking the silence over the dark, softly-rippling water. Gliding along gently, she noticed the occasional light shining in a window set high in the peeling wall of a canal-side hotel, or from the many low bridges straddling the water. And Marco laughed at her gasp of amazement when the gondolier appeared to duck his head in the nick of time as they passed beneath.

'Renato has travelled these waterways all his life. He never makes a mistake,' Marco told her, sliding his arm along the back of her seat, his hand gently covering her shoulder as he drew her towards him. 'Later, we shall return by way of the Canal Grande when it will be brightly lit and busy, in contrast to this stretch of water.'

'It's just wonderful,' she declared with a happy sigh. 'I couldn't have wished for anything nicer on my birthday.'

'Tell me,' he asked softly, 'is it proving to be as romantic as you anticipated?'

'Oh, yes, much more romantic than the waterboats. They're always so crowded.'

He nodded thoughtfully.

'Yes, I often watch them from my window, laden with people, heading in all directions. Tell me, Kathrine, in which direction are you heading? What do you expect from life?'

'Oh, Marco, what a question!' she exclaimed laughingly. 'I couldn't possibly give you an answer without giving it more thought.'

'But you are young and pretty,' he observed. 'There must be someone special who shares your romantic aspirations, who awaits your return.'

She gave an emphatic shake of her head.

'No, I've told you before, no-one. Why do you ask?'

He smiled and drew her closer until her

head rested against his shoulder.

'I needed to know,' he whispered, causing her a shiver of pleasure. 'I haven't been able to get you out of my thoughts since you arrived. I want to know everything about you, Kathrine—your work, and the accident, what happens in your life.'

Lost for words, Kate remained silent when, to her relief, the gondolier began to sing, his clear voice rising on the warm, evening air. She was beginning to appreciate just how easily this unique city could capture the heart of an unsuspecting visitor, just as Marco had predicted. But what would he have to say if he were to learn of the cloud of suspicion she had been under, the reason she'd felt obliged to leave her employment? In addition to that, there remained the possibility Greg would incriminate her in the claim for damages resulting from his reckless driving.

'An old Italian love song which Renato sings so very beautifully,' Marco commented, bringing her thoughts back to the present as the singer's voice rose to end the song in a long, high note.

After a brief exchange with Marco, the gondolier pulled over to a mooring and hopped ashore, his sudden movement rocking the slender craft.

'I have asked Renato to return later,' Marco told her. 'There is a small restaurant nearby and not too many people realise its existence so it is both quiet and unspoiled.'

He indicated a narrow, dimly-lit alley a short distance ahead and rose to help her ashore. Hand in hand they walked along the path beside the canal, to where the restaurant was situated in a tiny square. Once inside, they were shown to a table in a secluded alcove where candle-light provided a soft, intimate glow. Seated opposite, Marco translated the menu and explained the dishes, helping her to make her choice.

'What a cosy little restaurant,' she remarked after he had given their order, 'and so very Italian.'

'Venetian,' he corrected gently. 'Only local dishes are cooked here.'

Raising his glass, he drank a toast to her birthday, his gaze lingering upon her across the table.

When the first course arrived, Marco was unable to suppress his amusement as she attempted to copy the deft manner with which he tackled a plateful of spaghetti. Laughingly, she allowed him to instruct her in the art of twirling the long strands into manageable mouthfuls.

'You learn quickly,' he commented with a chuckle. 'Did you enjoy it?'

Kate was about to reply when the murmur of other diners was drowned by a shriek of female laughter followed by the sound of breaking glass.

'Tourists?' she queried with an amused glance.

Marco uttered a sigh of annoyance.

'No, I think not,' he said coolly when the woman's voice demanded the cost of the breakages be charged to the Ferrari account.

'And order a motoscafo, there's a good guy,' Kate heard a male voice demand in the pseudo-American drawl she instantly recognised.

Glancing sideways she saw Camilla, closely followed by the unmistakable form of Jonathan Webb. Her heart sank when she realised they were heading in their direction, Camilla's dark beauty and flame coloured dress catching everyone's attention as she swept along.

'Marco!' Camilla exclaimed as she drew near. 'And Miss . . . er . . . I am forgetting your name,' she ended with the briefest of glances at Kate.

Marco rose and murmured a polite greeting to include Camilla's escort who hovered a short distance behind.

'You should have told me you were here,' Camilla continued in a petulant tone. 'We could have dined together.'

'Katherine and I were discussing Venetian cuisine,' Marco told her in a reasonably pleasant tone.

Camilla wrinkled her nose.

'How terribly boring for you, caro.'

Marco broke into a torrent of Italian which Kate couldn't possibly follow. But she did realise he was growing extremely angry and only seconds passed before Camilla swept out of the restaurant, followed by the scowling Jonathan Webb. Quickly regaining his composure, Marco returned to his seat, spreading his hands in a gesture of despair.

'Again, I find myself apologising for Camilla's rudeness. I notice her American friend made no comment so I assume he doesn't speak Italian.'

'Please, don't feel responsible,' she said, and wondered if she should admit to the possibility she was already acquainted with Webb, but Webb had been so insistent they had not met, she might appear foolish if she mentioned it now.

'I'm afraid I do,' he said, his hand covering hers briefly, 'and I will not allow your evening to be spoiled by anyone.'

Kate shot him a quick smile and attempted to continue as if nothing had happened, but however charming an escort Marco continued to be, she noticed a certain tension about his manner and a lack of humour in his inscrutable blue eyes as the evening progressed. On the return journey along the wide canal between floodlit churches and palaces, Marco's arm rested casually across the seat behind her, his hand only tightening on hers to help her to her feet when the gondola drew alongside the bridge by the palazzo. He had seemed rather preoccupied since dinner, and she was certain Camilla was responsible.

CHAPTER FIVE

Kate had hardly dared to hope for Marco's telephone call which came the following morning, and when she hesitated over his invitation to take her sightseeing, it was almost as if he read her thoughts.

'Camilla is busy organising the exhibition so it is unlikely she will be around,' he assured her.

A short time later, they were strolling from room to room in the Accademia where she saw the masterpieces of Tintoretto, Veronese and many other famous artists. With Marco beside her to explain their history in detail, her appreciation grew.

'Of course, you can't expect to view all the works displayed in one visit, but we shall come again,' he promised, about to continue when someone tapping on the office window caught his attention.

'Will you excuse me, Kathrine? The secretary would like a word about the exhibition,' he explained. 'I'll be with you in a few minutes.'

He directed her towards another room to

view a compelling Veronese canvas which covered an entire wall. Content to continue, she followed the arrows indicating the route visitors should take. But when she turned into the next room she came to a sudden halt, finding herself facing Greg.

'What are you doing here?' she demanded, the colour draining from her face. 'You have no right to pester me.'

'Pester you?' he derided. 'Oh, Kate, what kind of welcome is this?'

'What do you expect?' she retaliated. 'I thought you would have gone home by now.'

'No, not yet. We're in a spot of bother,' he said, 'or perhaps I should say, you are.'

'Exactly what is that supposed to mean?'

'It's rather a long story,' he told her, handing her a card. 'I've booked into a hotel not far from here, so meet me there tonight when I'll have more time to explain,' then on a cryptic note he went on to add, 'You see, they've issued a summons, and you're involved.'

He hesitated, his grin widening as he noted her stunned expression.

'I'll fill in the details later. See you there around seven.'

Kate stared after Greg's retreating figure in dismay, and she barely had a chance to gather her wits before she heard Marco's voice coming in her direction. She thrust the card into her bag.

'You didn't get very far,' he observed with a smile. 'Which picture captured your attention?'

'I've taken my time with them all,' she managed with forced enthusiasm, 'but perhaps that one is my favourite.'

'Yes, it's quite beautiful,' he agreed. 'Are you ready to move on?'

She nodded, and they left to go in the direction of Saint Mark's Square to view the Doge's Palace with its impressive stairway rising from the courtyard, and the Great Council Chamber above.

'You're very quiet, Kathrine. Is something troubling you?' he paused to ask as they came back into the open.

'No, I'm fine,' she assured him quickly, 'just a little overawed, maybe, but I'm glad you're here to explain everything.'

'The pleasure is mine,' he said, squeezing her hand gently. 'Perhaps you would like to look round my home after lunch. It also represents a tiny piece of the history of this city.'

'Thank you, I'd love to,' she agreed without hesitation. 'My aunt has told me about your fabulous art collection, and the lovely Venetian glass.'

He smiled over her enthusiasm.

'But first we shall enjoy a quiet meal together,' he decided, 'then you may take your time looking around.'

To Kate's dismay, the quiet lunch Marco proposed didn't turn out as planned. They had only just made a start on their first course when the dining-room door burst open and Camilla rushed in, followed closely by Marco's manservant who hovered anxiously in the doorway.

'Marco, I have to see you,' Camilla said, ignoring Kate completely as she went to his side. 'If I'm to move freely around the palazzo to arrange this exhibition I shall need your keys. Georgio seems reluctant to part with his without your permission. Will you speak with him, caro?'

With a brief nod, Marco dismissed his manservant, and turning to Camilla, he asked coolly, 'Couldn't this have waited until later? I had planned to take Kathrine round the palazzo after lunch.'

'But what about me!' Camilla exclaimed furiously. 'You know how awkward Georgio can be, and I can't think of lunch with this on my mind!'

'Sit down and be quiet!' he directly sternly. 'Starving yourself won't solve anything, and I think you owe Kathrine an apology for this interruption.'

Camilla appeared to resign herself to the fact that Marco wasn't to be moved by her angry display, and, forcing a brief smile in Kate's direction, she sank down on a chair.

'Forgive me,' she said, spreading her red-tipped fingers, 'I should not depend upon Marco so much.'

Kate acknowledged this with a stiff smile but as the meal continued she found it to be less enjoyable than she had anticipated. It wasn't the food, which was delicious, it was Camilla's incessant chatter dampening her appetite. But Marco reminded the dark beauty to include Kate in the conversation. He had spoken sharply in Italian, but by Camilla's petulant response Kate guessed what he had said.

'Is preparing for an exhibition hard work?' Kate asked the woman politely when the ensuing silence had become almost impossible to endure.

Camilla gave a harsh laugh.

'Hard work, yes! But I enjoy it if it is for someone special,' she replied.

To this Marco merely raised his dark brows. Kate was relieved when the meal came to an end so that she could take her leave, suggesting she come to view the palazzo another day. But he wouldn't hear of it and took her on the promised tour of the vast number of rooms, each containing remarkable pieces of Venetian glass and antique furniture.

Descending to the lower apartments surrounding the courtyard, they had just reached the foot of the steps when Georgio caught their attention from the direction of the rear entrance.

'Rose wishes to speak with you,' Marco translated after his short exchange with Georgio. 'I have asked him to allow her to bring the message to you personally.'

Murmuring her thanks, Kate looked expectantly towards the doorway to see Rose crossing the courtyard.

'Signorina, there is a gentleman on the telephone who wishes to speak with you,' the girl announced breathlessly.

Going towards Rosa, Kate frowned.

'Are you sure? I wasn't expecting anyone to call.'

'But it is your fiancé, Signore Courtney,' Rose said.

Kate came to a sudden halt and gaped at the smiling girl.

'My what? Courtney, did you say?'

'Si, Si, your fiancé. He is waiting to speak with you.'

'But he's not my fiancé!' she stammered as she turned to meet Marco's cold stare.

'Come, come, Kathrine, don't keep the girl dithering here,' he cut in. 'Your fiancé is waiting!'

And with that final icy reminder he swung round on his heel and quickly mounted the stairs.

'You are happy to speak with Signore Courtney, no?' the maid asked as they left by way of the stone bridge.

'No!' Kate almost sobbed, but seeing Rosa's

crestfallen look, added quickly, 'But you did right to let me know.'

'I usually answer the telephone when Signora Rossini is resting,' the girl explained and Kate knew that if her aunt had taken the call she would have dealt with Greg herself.

As they walked the short distance to her aunt's house she recalled Marco's icy stare of only moments before and her heart sank. What could he have thought? Dismally, she entered the house and made her way slowly upstairs to pick up the telephone.

'Just a reminder, be at my hotel at seven, or else,' she heard Greg say before she slammed down the receiver.

That evening, seated opposite Greg in the lounge of his hotel, she saw his old confidence return, the gleam of triumph in his eyes irritating her almost beyond endurance.

'Well, what was it you wanted to tell me?' she prompted sharply. 'My only reason for being here is to discover why the summons concerns me.'

'Before we discuss that, have a glass of wine,' he suggested. 'I don't want you having hysterics.'

'Which is most unlikely,' she responded coolly, concealing the tension she felt. 'In fact, I'm beginning to think this is just a ruse to get me here.'

'You won't say that when you see the papers I brought with me, but that will keep. Now, what will you have?' he asked, signalling the waiter. 'I'm not discussing anything until I've had a drop of wine.'

Despairingly, Kate selected a drink, and waited with increasing apprehension for the time when he would choose to enlighten her. Finally, she took a steadying breath.

'I understand we are here because you have something to tell me, so will you please get on with it,' she reminded him.

'We can't discuss it here,' he said curtly, rising to his feet. 'Come with me. The papers are in my room.'

'Then you can bring them down,' she directed. 'I can read them here.'

'Don't be stupid,' he retorted. 'They're private.'

He came round to draw back her chair, indicating for her to follow him from the dining-room to the brightly-lit reception area where he asked for his key. With mounting trepidation, Kate waited a short distance from the desk whilst the receptionist attended to Greg. Somehow, she doubted he was being frank with her yet would he have come all this way unless the matter was serious?

She was just reminding herself to be on her guard when the sound of a familiar female voice caught her attention and she quickly averted her head just as Greg strolled up, his room key swinging from his finger.

'As you're so impatient, let's go,' he said,

ushering Kate ahead of him as he turned towards the stairs.

Imagining the impression Camilla would have seeing them go upstairs together, she hesitated at the door of Greg's room.

'I think it would be wiser to discuss this downstairs. The lounge was almost empty.'

'I'm not going to eat you!' he exclaimed, grinning as he turned the key and indicated for her to enter. 'Anyway, I'd like to know more about this Italian pal of yours.'

'I thought you already knew, after all, your friend Webb was at the palazzo the other evening.'

'Don't know anyone of that name,' he denied and hurried on to say, 'I'd like to get a look at Ferrari's place, you know, do a spot of socialising. Any chance of you getting me in?'

'Certainly not! Greg, you really are the limit, and if I have any say in the matter I'll advise Marco against letting you in, so you'd have to ask him yourself.'

'Marco, is it? You haven't wasted much time. Actually, I thought you could find a way for me to have a look round. I'm interested in these old buildings but I can't be bothered with formal introductions. I notice Ferrari appears to enjoy a luxurious lifestyle, but I thought all those musty old palaces had been turned into museums.'

'Not this one. I've seen it myself and it's beautiful!' she returned crossly, then with a sigh of impatience reminded him, 'But I'm not here to talk about palaces, particularly when they're private.'

His eyes narrowed.

'But if I were to drop a hint about why you lost your job in England, I think he'd welcome me with open arms.'

'You wouldn't dare! I've a good mind to tell . . .'

He held up a silencing finger, and his lip curled in a sneer as he returned sharply, 'Ah, but you won't, not after you've heard what I've got to say.'

'Well, for goodness' sake get on with it. I'm tired of hearing your voice.'

'Ah, yes, the papers,' he said, withdrawing them from his briefcase, handing one to her. 'Read this first. It's the summons I received.'

'But it doesn't concern me!' she cried incredulously. 'Surely you haven't brought me here for that!'

'Then you may find this fax from my solicitor more interesting,' he returned with a sneer. 'And perhaps now you will listen to me.'

Kate's initial feelings of disbelief were quickly dispelled when he confronted her with the copy of the typewritten sheet. It appeared Greg was contesting the summons for cost of the damage he'd caused on the grounds he wasn't driving the vehicle at the time of the accident, naming Kate as the person who was.

'But you were driving!' she cried, completely

aghast. 'Surely you're not going to put the blame on me. I wasn't in the driving seat.'

He looked at her and grinned.

'If you remember, I was rather tipsy at the time, so I had to stick to my original story. In addition to that, I have no chance whatsoever of meeting those costs, plus my licence is already endorsed. You'd get away with it easily,' he continued with confidence. 'You know the owner of the building. Make an offer for compensation and say you were blinded by the lights of an oncoming vehicle, a dog ran out, or some such tale. You'll think of something.'

'But the road was deserted!' she gasped. 'And besides that, I haven't a licence.'

'You damned fool!' he cried. 'Why didn't you tell me this before?'

'You never asked,' she replied quickly, and reminded him, 'Anyway, you always said you would never trust women drivers!'

He calmed a little.

'Well, I suppose that could mean you'll get a small fine. At least you haven't a licence to lose.'

'Now look here, I didn't agree to you saying I was driving,' she returned hotly. 'You'd already told them that before I was fully conscious.'

He gave a hiss of impatience.

'Damn it, Kate, I had to give some sort of explanation, but I didn't think we'd hear anything further.'

'No, Greg, you, not we,' she intervened sharply. 'I've suffered quite enough without having to lie for you as well.'

'Come on, sweetheart,' he cajoled, reaching for her hand. 'I know you won't let an old friend down.'

'Some friend!' she cried bitterly. 'Tell me, where were you during the time I was in hospital? No, Greg, you're, no friend of mine so you can count me out!'

He caught up with her as she reached the door, and forcing a smile on his flushed face said, 'Surely, you're not going to turn against me now.'

'Get out of my way!' she hissed, pushing him aside. 'If you try to stop me I'll scream the place down.'

'You'll regret this!' came the harsh response, his smiling expression quickly fading. 'Just you wait!'

Ignoring him, Kate hurried in the direction of the stairs, her anxiety increasing as his threats penetrated her troubled thoughts. What was she to do if Greg persisted with this story? And would anyone believe her should she deny it? She made her way back to the house, unhappily contemplating the steps she must take to prevent Greg involving her in this case.

* * *

'I can't imagine what Marco must have thought when Rose announced Greg as my fiancé,' Kate said as she faced her aunt across the breakfast table the following morning. 'I've got to give some sort of explanation, otherwise he may get the wrong impression.'

Signora Rossini nodded.

'I agree, he's bound to think it rather strange. Marco's reaction has really upset you, hasn't it?' she ended shrewdly.

'Yes, it has,' she admitted, though reluctant to mention the reason Greg had phoned.

She saw no point in involving her aunt in the matter of the summons, confident she could deal with it herself. But now, as she made her way to the palazzo, she could think of no suitable way to explain the call.

'Buon giorno,' she said brightly when Georgio opened the door. 'I would like to see Signore Ferrari.'

'The signore is working at his desk,' the man replied, inclining his head briefly as he beckoned her inside.

Thanking him, she made her way up the wide staircase, glancing down on the courtyard below as she reflected on how her opportunity to see the lower rooms and boathouse had been so dramatically interrupted. Fear rose within her as she recalled Marco's icy expression at the time. But it also added strength to her determination to put things right between them, and remembering which was Marco's study from her tour of the first floor, she knocked on the solid wooden door.

'Entri!' a voice commanded and she drew a steadying breath before entering the room to find him engrossed in the papers on his desk.

'Si?' he said, without glancing up.

'Good morning,' she murmured shakily and noticed his hand stiffen.

He continued writing for a few seconds before he slowly raised his head. As he got to his feet she met his stony gaze and continued hopefully.

'I'd like a word with you, if you're not too busy.'

He sighed and gestured to the papers before him.

'I do have a great deal of work to get through before lunch,' he said tersely. 'Can't it wait?'

'I only intend taking a little of your time,' she replied, gathering courage. 'You see, I feel I must explain.'

'There's no need for you to explain anything, Kathrine,' he broke in. 'I believe we concluded our tour of Venice so you are at liberty to spend the remainder of your holiday just how you wish. You are under no obligation.'

'Please, allow me to explain!' she cried in dismay. 'I didn't know Greg would phone me here.'

'Greg? Your fiancé?'

'He's not my fiancé. He was just being stupid,' she said, forcing a smile. 'In fact, I was furious with him for interrupting my visit. I was really looking forward to seeing the boat-house and . . .'

'Perhaps another time,' he broke in without enthusiasm, returning his attention to the desk. 'I believe you have already made another friend.'

'Friend?' she said blankly, then exhaled slowly as it dawned on her what he meant. 'Oh, you mean the man at the hotel? No, that was Greg, but I assure you I won't be seeing him again.'

He glanced up slowly, fixing her with an icy-blue stare.

'Why?' he demanded, the vehemence of his tone startling her. 'Is he not satisfactory?'

'How dare you!' she gasped. 'How dare you infer there is anything between us? You are the most presumptuous . . .'

'Presumptuous!' he echoed, his lips curling disdainfully as he leaned towards her. 'I understand you were willing to go to this man's room, so I consider my presumptions are well founded.'

'I was what?' she cried, meeting his stony expression.

He held up his hand.

'Please, spare me the need to repeat this sordid information.'

'But if you will only let me explain.'

'I prefer not to discuss your personal adventures,' he said coldly before he quickly turned away from her to go and stare through the window.

The heated colour left her face.

'I'll bet your informant almost choked over her dinner in her hurry to bring that tit-bit of gossip to you!'

Marco spun away from the window.

'So, tell me, what am I to think?'

'If only you would listen,' she reproached brokenly. 'I left the hotel soon after Camilla saw me, but you haven't given me the chance to explain.'

'Maybe not,' he admitted. 'Quite frankly, I was angry. I understood you to be unattached.'

Her heart gave a tiny jolt.

'And is that important to you?' she queried, her head held high.

For a long moment he merely held her gaze then, as if to avoid the question, said, 'Naturally, I wouldn't wish to cause any friction between you and this friend of yours by imposing upon your time. Even so, I had no right to lose my temper.'

'Quite,' she murmured on a note of disappointment, 'but, as I told you before, he is no particular friend of mine.'

'Yet you are still acquainted with this man?' he queried quietly, his dark brows lifting.

'I was,' she replied with emphasis, 'but that

70

is all in the past. Even so,' she continued as she reached for the door handle, 'I don't wish to impose upon your time by discussing my personal life.'

CHAPTER SIX

Kate's heart was heavy as she left the palazzo to hurry along the canal side. Marco had apologised, but there was a coolness in his manner towards her, and all because of Greg. She had considered revealing the reason for her meeting with him but, as she was in no way responsible for the accident, felt it was not necessary for her to explain.

She also had thought of mentioning her suspicions regarding Webb, but since Greg appeared ignorant as to whom she was referring, she had begun to wonder if her memory deceived her. However, although she hadn't realised it at the time, another matter had become clear. Greg had been aware of her visits to the palazzo but, unless Webb had told him, how could he know?

Once she was well away from the palazzo her pace slowed. She was enveloped by a feeling of despair over both her friendship with Marco and Greg's intention to involve her in the summons. When she finally returned home, hopeful of going to her room unobserved, Signora Rossini waylaid her to enquire if she had seen Marco.

'Yes,' she managed with forced lightness, 'and I've been for a stroll.'

'With Marco?'

'No, but in this lovely weather it seemed a shame to be indoors,' she rushed on then faltered, knowing tears were imminent.

'Oh, my dear!' the signora exclaimed gently. 'Come, tell me what troubles you.'

'I'm sorry,' Kate said, fumbling for her handkerchief. 'I'd rather not discuss it.'

'Just as you wish, but I assume I'm correct in thinking Marco was not too happy with your explanation of Greg's presence.'

Brushing away her tears, Kate nodded.

'He wasn't. In fact, he was quite insulting so I don't know why I'm allowing myself to get so upset about it.'

'A typical Latin reaction. He's jealous!' her aunt declared with satisfaction. 'Exactly what did he say?'

'It seems Camilla saw me go up to Greg's room at his hotel. Obviously, she exaggerated the situation, so he now presumes I spent the night there.'

The signora clicked her tongue reprovingly.

'But going to Greg's room was rather foolish, particularly after you told me it was over between you.'

'It is, and it wasn't anything like that. You must believe me.'

'I do, but did you convince Marco you and Greg are not . . . er . . . lovers?'

Kate sighed.

'I don't know, but when the time comes for me to go home, I'd hate to leave with him having a bad opinion of me. It's so unjust.'

'But you still haven't explained why you went to Greg's room in the first place,' the signora pointed out.

'I only went to look at some papers he had with him, nothing more.'

The signora cast her a shrewd glance.

'Concerning the accident?'

Kate gave a guilty start.

'How did you know?'

'I think I'm right in assuming there was far more to that accident than you've admitted.'

Kate sighed.

'In a way, yes, but nothing you should worry about.'

The signora threw up her hands in exasperation.

'Of course I shall worry, unless you care to tell me about it.'

'I feel I must tell someone,' Kate confessed in a shaky voice and reluctantly related the latest development in the matter of the pending summons, ending on a sorrowful note. 'And Greg has such a plausible tongue, who's going to believe me?'

Signora Rossini nodded thoughtfully.

'Mm, somehow, he's got to be made to own

up, though I don't like the sound of the threat he made. What possible connection could it have with your last employer?'

Kate sank into a nearby chair.

'I suppose you may as well know,' she began with a sigh. 'As you may be aware, I had taken a private post, nursing a lady who was terminally ill, and I really enjoyed working there. It was a perfect place to live, a beautiful house and gardens, and I got on with the family really well.'

'Why did you leave? Were they not nice people to work for?'

Kate pursed her lips for a moment, then went on.

'Yes, but then something occurred and I felt obliged to leave. You see, something quite valuable went missing and suspicion fell on me.'

'Oh, Kate, surely they didn't suspect you of stealing?'

'They didn't actually accuse me, they had no proof, but their manner towards me changed. I wouldn't dream of stealing from a patient.'

'I know that, but what an awful situation this must have been for you, and then for Greg to bring it up again now.'

Although Kate experienced some relief at unburdening herself, she still felt dismayed over Marco's hurtful remarks. Whatever reason her aunt had provided to excuse his behaviour, it didn't help to ease the fact his manner was now less friendly towards her. Why did it trouble her so much, she asked herself repeatedly as sleep eluded her that night. Could she be falling in love with this handsome Venetian?

Kate spent the following two days indoors, reluctant to go out in case she should encounter Greg. But, when Friday came, she agreed to accompany her aunt to the home of a close friend who lived on the other side of the Grand Canal.

The beautiful house they visited was not unlike the palazzo, though smaller, and it was only when the guests had assembled to go in to dinner that she caught sight of Marco across the room. Her heart gave a tiny lurch when she realised he was heading their way, and very soon he was standing beside them, tall and immaculate in a white dinner jacket.

'Signora Margaret, Signorina Kathrine,' he greeted them, smiling as he took her aunt's hand, though merely raising a dark brow in Kate's direction. 'I trust you are well?'

Kate gave him a tremulous smile, while her aunt immediately entered into conversation, issuing Marco with an invitation to lunch the following week.

'Unfortunately, I shall be away,' he said with a shrug of reluctance. 'I have business in Florence, but possibly the following week-end?'

'Of course, Marco, perhaps you will contact

me on your return,' the signora suggested then, as though it had just occurred to her, went on to say, 'Kate tells me she has not yet seen your wonderful paintings, or the boathouse. She was most disappointed to miss the opportunity last time, weren't you, dear?' she prompted, turning to her niece.

'Oh, I don't expect you to . . .' Kate began, but he raised a silencing hand.

'Why not join me for tea tomorrow?' he invited, and before she had a chance to decline, went on to insist, 'I'll expect you both around four.'

Kate's opportunity to resist was thwarted when the glamorous figure of Camilla appeared at his side.

'Ah, caro, you are here,' the woman purred, flashing her dark eyes in Marco's direction before she turned to Kate to enquire casually, 'Your fiancé is not here this evening, Miss Macleod? I was hoping to meet him.'

'Sorry to disappoint you, but I don't have a fiancé,' Kate returned, her manner equally casual, and taking her aunt's arm, suggested, 'Perhaps we should find our seats.'

Throughout dinner, although seated some distance from Marco, there were times when she could sense his eyes resting upon her and wondered what was in his thoughts. Had he felt obliged to invite them to tea tomorrow merely because her aunt had reminded him her previous visit to the palazzo had been curtailed, or had he extended the invitation in the hope of seeing her again? She wouldn't have thought him the kind of man who needed to arrange some social occasion purely to satisfy his wishes. He was far too self-assured for that.

The meal seemed endless and she had to make an effort to concentrate on the conversation around her as they relaxed over coffee. When at last it was time to leave, she breathed a sigh of relief. Being in the same room as Marco, with Camilla at his side, had made the occasion almost unbearable.

The next day, promptly at four, Kate and her aunt presented themselves at the palazzo. Wishing to keep the occasion informal, Marco had arranged for tea to be served in a small, comfortable salon overlooking the courtyard. The main topic of conversation was the weather forecast when he expressed his anxiety over the storm warning and the possibility of flooding as a result.

His expression was serious as he said, 'I dislike the thought of being out of Venice should this occur.'

The signora voiced her own dismay.

'It worries me, too, but I'll keep my eye on things as usual whilst you're away. Don't forget to leave the telephone number of your hotel.'

'I'll take my mobile with me. You have that number.'

Immediately tea was over, Marco suggested

they go and view his more valuable paintings which were hanging in a room just off his study near the head of the rear staircase.

'I don't like having to keep them hidden away like this,' he said as he went ahead to unlock the door. 'Such beauty should be available for all to see. They will be on show at the exhibition when I'm at home, and as you know I am in the process of having alarms fitted. Meanwhile, until I can ensure their safety outside this room, viewing is reserved for close friends.'

Kate gazed in wonderment at the pictures hanging there, some framed in heavy gilt, beautiful scenes of Venice, the Italian lakes and mountains, and others in plain dark frames which, he told her, were the most valuable of the collection. A few of the painters were known to her, but others, many of them priceless works, were not, yet Marco could relate their history in detail.

'It is like having, your own art gallery,' she said with a sigh of admiration as they left the room. 'You must feel very proud to own such a collection.'

'I enjoy having beautiful things around me,' he said with a smile as he locked the door, 'but I would like to share my pleasure with others. Once the fitting of alarms has been completed and in working order, I intend moving them into the grand salon.'

He tossed the key into the drawer of his

desk.

'Unfortunately, such drastic measures are necessary as paintings can so easily go missing. To improve security is the only way.'

She nodded.

'Yes, indeed, as you say, more people can enjoy them that way. But I thought you already allow certain visitors to look around the palazzo.'

'Only historians, or those who are really interested in our architecture,' he told her as they left his study to go towards the stairs. 'Only when I'm here, of course, and always by appointment.'

'Very wise,' she agreed as they descended the steps, the same route she had taken on that terrible day when Rosa had come into the courtyard below to announce Greg's telephone call, but now, with Marco guiding her attention to the area of the palazzo which was new to her, she cast aside that awful memory and listened to what he had to say.

'These are the servants' quarters,' he explained when they reached the ground floor, 'or rather, they were in years gone by. Now we are more considerate and put them on a higher level so they do not have to worry about the floods.'

'Does the water rise so high?' she asked in amazement as she looked into the dimly-lit rooms, shuddering in the cool atmosphere.

He laughed at her incredulous expression.

'Sometimes, in the spring when the tides are high,' he told her as he led the way over the stone-floored courtyard.

To the right of the rear entrance, under a vaulted ceiling leading towards the boathouse, stood an old gondola, its ornamental trappings green with age. It reminded Kate of films she had seen of the past when lovers took refuge in such a vessel, stealing unseen kisses as they glided along.

'It was used by my family years ago,' Marco said as he beckoned her towards a heavy, wooden door at the end of the wide passage and drew back the huge, metal bolt. 'In the past, most families owned their own gondolas but now usually they hire one. But now let us turn to modern means of transport. Come, see where I keep the launch,' he said and swung the door wide, standing aside for her to enter.

Down a short flight of steps, Kate's eyes travelled along the ceiling which fell to a mere seven or eight feet, and a floor sloping to a water-filled cavern below where daylight filtered in through a rusting iron grille. The heavy grille dropped below water level, protecting the palazzo from intruders. And there, in the water, lay Marco's launch, its gentle buffeting increasing each time boats passed on the canal outside.

'It looks very deep,' she commented, her voice echoing eerily round the damp stone chamber.

'Not so deep as when the floods are with us,' he told her. 'The entrance is completely obliterated, so all boats must be left tied up outside.'

Kate shuddered and turned away.

'I can understand why you are concerned over the weather forecast, particularly as you will be away. When exactly do you expect to return?'

He shrugged.

'Friday, at the earliest. I have a number of meetings to attend.'

'But won't Georgio be here if the waters rise? I expect he's used to it.'

'I've agreed to Georgio taking a few days to visit his sister in Padua,' he disclosed as they made to leave the watery cavern.

'You leave this huge place unattended?' she asked in surprise.

'Why not?' he queried. 'It is quite secure.'

And to add emphasis to his statement he drove the bolt in the heavy door firmly home.

'So I see.'

She laughed as they retraced their steps to where Signora Rossini waited.

It was just after Kate had thanked him for the interesting tour that Marco suggested a visit to the Isle of Murano the following day. Suppressing a surge of delight, she merely smiled.

'But you're going away on business,' she reminded him.

'Not until Monday, so tomorrow is a day for pleasure,' he said, casting the signora a questioning glance.

'Not for me, Marco. I intend to rest,' the signora protested laughingly, 'but I'm sure Kate will enjoy it.'

Turning to Kate, he raised a dark brow.

'So, it is just the two of us, yes?' He smiled. 'Can you be ready soon after lunch?'

CHAPTER SEVEN

Immediately after lunch the following day they set off in Marco's launch. During the morning Kate had been undecided about taking this trip. After all, only the previous week Marco had more or less stated his services as guide were no longer available, so she found his present attitude confusing. However, her spirits rose to the welcome breeze which swept over her as they left the busy canal to cross the lagoon.

'I am sure you will find it interesting,' he said as they disembarked. 'We can visit both the Guistinian Palace, and one of the factories.'

'I'm sure I shall. It is something I've not seen before,' she agreed.

'Our glass-manufacturing industry is world famous, dating back to the thirteenth century,' he told her. 'The heat of the furnaces must have been almost unbearable at that time.'

Standing on an earthen floor, fanning herself with her straw hat, Kate watched the craftsman. She was amazed to see how deftly he manipulated the rod he held after he drew it from the furnace to urge its tip of molten glass into the desired shape.

'Oh, Marco, just look at that!' she cried, marvelling at the final result.

'A skill which comes from years of practice,' he said. 'Are you pleased we came?'

She shot him a smiling glance.

'Of course, though I must admit I was surprised you suggested it. Not that I didn't wish to come,' she hastened to add, 'but after what you said in your office . . .'

'Unfortunately, I allowed myself to presume too much on that occasion,' he admitted a trifle stiffly. 'However, with the hope you will forgive my momentary weakness, perhaps we can continue as before.'

'Of course,' she murmured.

Once their tour of Murano was completed, they returned to where the launch was moored.

'I suggest we return to Venice for refreshment as it looks like rain is on the way,' Marco commented as he helped her aboard.

Kate glanced up, observing the swiftly-moving clouds.

'Have we time to call in that little café

where we had the accident in your launch? The man was so kind, I'd like to thank him.'

'Most certainly, though I have already called to assure him you were not seriously harmed.'

Just off the Grand Canal they tied up at the same mooring they had used on the previous occasion. They entered the small café which stood back from the water's edge just as the rain began to fall quite heavily.

'Signore, signorina!' the proprietor gushed, rushing forward to greet them. 'I have news for you!' he said excitedly, leading them to a table in a secluded corner of the room.

After Marco had ordered, he reverted to his familiar tongue when Kate lost gist of the conversation. She saw Marco's brows rise enquiringly as he spoke to the proprietor, then noticed the latter's excited response when he nodded in the direction of the canal outside and gestured expressively as he glanced her way. She assumed they discussed the accident and understood the word meaning boat. But when the word, Verdi, was spoken, she noticed Marco frown. Marco then spread his hands resignedly and sighed, causing her curiosity to increase. Perhaps it wasn't the collision they spoke of after all, but Camilla. She needed to clarify the Italian woman's place in his affections for her own peace of mind.

'I've been meaning to ask you about Camilla,' she ventured when the proprietor had left their table. 'Does she spend all her time working on art exhibitions?'

'Not all her time. Organising fashion shows and cocktail parties plays quite a large part, and the odd art exhibition is fitted in when there's time.'

'I wonder where she met Jonathan Webb,' Kate pursued thoughtfully. 'Have you any idea?'

'No, can't help you there. But Camilla loves mixing with the rich and famous, so maybe he fits into that category,' he said with a smile. 'Why do you ask?'

Kate avoided his question and remarked, 'She's still young so I expect she enjoys her return to social life.'

He laughed quietly.

'During her period of mourning she rarely left the house then, quite suddenly, in the past six months, her feet haven't touched the ground.'

'Do you think she'll marry again?'

The laughter faded from his eyes as he said, 'Camilla possesses a temperament which is most impetuous, and also rather . . .'

'Possessive?' Kate ventured a trifle apprehensively.

'What makes you say that, Kathrine?'

'Well, she appears quite possessive where you're concerned,' she declared. 'In fact, I get the distinct impression she resents me being in your company, so I hope it doesn't cause trouble between you.'

It was a moment before he replied.

'I shall be relieved when the time comes for me to hand over my responsibilities,' he said. 'My degree in law came in very useful when she was widowed as her estate gave me many problems, but now everything is almost settled.'

'Oh, I see,' she murmured, barely managing to conceal her relief. 'Then she's fortunate to have the benefit of your advice.'

She was about to ask about the boat which struck the launch when last they were here, but then, with a half smile, Marco reached for her hand across the table.

'Do I detect a hint of my own Latin failing in you, caro?' he asked softly. 'Are you also just a tiny bit jealous?'

'Oh, Marco,' she murmured, her cheeks growing warm, 'of course not.'

'I had hoped you were,' he groaned in mock dismay, his eyes sparkling mischievously, 'just a little.'

She smiled at him, only withdrawing her hand when the proprietor returned to ask if there was anything else they required.

'Grazie, no,' Marco replied pleasantly, thrusting some notes into the man's hand, and to Kate he suggested, 'I do believe the rain has stopped. Perhaps this is a good time to leave.'

'When do you leave tomorrow?' she asked as they reached the launch.

'Mid morning, I expect,' he said as he untied

the painter. 'Georgio will take me to the station and from there we will go our separate ways. Will you miss me?' he added softly as he drew her into the shelter of the wheelhouse.

Realising he was awaiting her reply, she admitted quietly, 'Yes, I expect I shall. I've enjoyed coming out with you today.'

He smiled and started the engine, taking the launch out to reach the wide canal in the direction of the palazzo. As they travelled along, she uttered a small sigh of contentment, knowing she would eagerly await his return.

'You could have dropped me off at the bridge,' she said as they left the boathouse to ascend the steps leading to the palazzo's upper floors. 'I'm sure you must have things to do before you leave tomorrow.'

'Georgio will have the packing finished by now so I am not in a hurry,' he said. 'And there is something I'd like you to have before you go.'

Curious, Kate followed him into the salon overlooking the canal. But, before Marco would enlighten her, he went to pour two glasses of wine.

'I have a small gift for you,' he said as he brought the drinks over, and taking a slim box from his pocket he handed it to her saying, 'I hope this will be a little more permanent than the one I gave to you on your birthday.'

Intrigued, she opened the box and there, beneath a layer of tissue, modelled in fine glass, lay a perfect red rosebud, its delicate stem and single leaf a realistic shade of green.

'Oh, it's really beautiful!' she exclaimed, putting down her bag to lift it carefully from the box. 'It's so lifelike I can almost smell it.'

'Just a little something to remind you of today,' he said in reply.

'Thank you, Marco, I shall treasure it.'

Smiling, he caught her chin in his warm hand, lifting her face to his when he sought her parted lips.

'I shall miss you,' he murmured as he raised his head, then drew away from her as footsteps sounded in the corridor outside.

A cloud of dismay descended upon Kate when she saw the figure in the doorway. After those last precious moments, the unexpected appearance of Camilla caused the surge of happiness she felt to fade.

'Ah, I see I am not the only one to call to wish you farewell, caro,' the woman declared, strolling across the room. 'But, of course, Kathrine being a special friend, that is different.'

Kate noticed the uncertain glance Marco sent her before he invited, 'Are you staying for drinks, Camilla?'

'It was my intention,' she replied, removing Kate's bag from the settee before seating herself in a most elegant pose before she went on to add, 'And I have arranged for my American friend to be brought here. He will not be long arriving. You must meet him again, Kathrine.'

Kate glanced at her watch but she knew it would appear impolite to leave now, before Jonathan got here. When he finally arrived, it took him some minutes to settle down.

'That kid of yours is crazy, Camilla!' he exclaimed breathlessly. 'At the speed that young devil travelled, we must have cut the time by half.'

Camilla laughed shrilly.

'That is how I like to travel. It is more exciting.'

'I don't like to think of him endangering your life, sweetheart,' Jonathan interrupted.

'Or anyone else's!' Marco interjected sharply. 'I've already reprimanded him about another incident.'

'Which incident, Marco?' Camilla inquired.

Marco frowned.

'I think you are already aware to which incident I am referring, Camilla.'

Camilla shrugged.

'No, caro, I have no idea, but I like a man with spirit.'

'Spirit!' Jonathan spluttered. 'It's a great wonder the golden hawk hadn't gotten washed off the bows the way he travels,' he declared, reverting to a steady drawl. 'Damn it, the kid's mad!'

Kate sensed Marco's quick glance in her direction. She was convinced this boat Webb spoke of with its golden crest was the same one which had struck them. And this, no doubt, would be the reason Marco had spoken to its helmsman.

Noticing the rain had started to fall again, Kate suggested it was time for her to leave and accepted Marco's offer to escort her over the bridge. Keeping a careful hold on the little box containing her souvenir she said farewell to the others while Marco went in search of an umbrella.

'I hope we can meet again when Marco returns,' Camilla said pleasantly. 'Perhaps dinner one evening?'

'Yes, perhaps,' Kate murmured, forcing a smile, though she doubted the sincerity behind the invitation.

At the door leading out to the enclosed garden, Marco drew her under the shelter of his umbrella.

'Mind where you tread,' he advised, guiding her carefully between the puddles when she enjoyed the close contact with his body.

As they entered the hallway of her aunt's home he set aside his umbrella, and took her hands.

'Keep Friday evening free, will you, Kathrine?' he asked softly before his lips met hers in a farewell kiss.

Immediately he left, Kate rushed upstairs hoping to catch a glimpse of him on the bridge below. It was as though he had sensed her presence at the window as he looked up, raising his hand to his lips in an affectionate salute. Friday seemed years away.

When he left next day, Kate watched as the launch pulled away from the palazzo, heading for the station with Marco and Georgio aboard. The canal looked distinctly grey, reflecting the cloud-laden sky on its choppy surface. She turned her thoughts away from Marco's leaving to Friday evening, the evening he requested she should keep free.

With a tiny smile of anticipation, she searched for something suitable to wear on such a gloomy day, planning to take a further look at the smaller shops away from the main square. But when she had finished dressing and looked for her little crocheted bag, it was nowhere to be found.

'I must have left it in the cloakroom at the palazzo,' she said when she joined her aunt in the main salon. 'I remember having it with me when we returned from Murano, but not when I came back here.'

'All you carried was the box containing the rose,' the signora reminded her, smiling. 'You were far too happy to care about anything else.'

'Never mind, it will have to stay there until he gets back. It contained nothing of great importance, but I'd hate to lose the bag.'

'It will be quite safe,' the signora assured her, but as Kate was leaving she raised a warning finger. 'I hope that Courtney fellow isn't hanging around. Do be careful, dear.'

Kate smiled.

'Don't worry, I will, though I expect he will have gone by now.'

Even so, the signora's reminder left her with a touch of anxiety so, instead of the quieter alleyways and squares, she chose the well-used thoroughfares only a short distance from Saint Mark's square.

She was nearing Marco's shop which sold the beautiful Venetian ornaments. She paused to look at the dazzling display from the safety of the pavement outside. As her gaze travelled over the items on show, she was suddenly aware of being observed from inside and glanced up to see the face of the assistant, Luigi, whom she'd met on the previous visits.

Now, unlike the earlier occasion, he grinned as he raised his hand in recognition. Giving him a rueful smile, she acknowledged him with a wave, and was just about to continue on her way when she was jerked to a sudden halt and confronted by the leer of triumph on Greg Courtney's face.

'Thought I'd find you alone, eventually,' he said with a mirthless laugh. 'Now your precious Marco's out of Venice we can have that little chat.'

'Take your hands off me!' she cried as she wrenched her arm away.

'I asked you to get me an introduction, you

know, a visit to his palace,' he said, reaching for her again. 'I expect he'll have left you with a key.'

'No, he hasn't,' she shrieked, 'and if he had I wouldn't give it to you.'

'Remember your reputation, Kate. He won't want to know you when he reads the letter I've sent him. Of course, if you have a key, I can easily get it back before he sees it.'

To Kate's immense relief, Luigi appeared in the doorway of the shop.

'Is this man troubling you, Miss Macleod?' he enquired, casting a thunderous look in Greg's direction 'Shall I call the police?'

'Thank you, I don't think that will be necessary,' she managed, stepping away from Greg. 'I think he knows he's wasting his time.'

Greg raised his hands in a protective pose.

'OK, OK, forget the police. I'm going. 'But as he turned away he hissed, 'This is not the end of it, Kate. If you won't play the game my way you can suffer the consequences!' Then he dashed off along the crowded street.

'Would you like to step inside?' Luigi invited, standing back for her to enter the shop. 'I expect he was after your money, but threatening to call the police soon sent him on his *way.*'

Shocked though she was, Kate managed a grateful smile.

'Yes, I expect you're right,' she agreed shakily, 'and I'm grateful for your intervention, but I don't think he will trouble me again.' With a short laugh she added, 'Anyway, perhaps it will be safer if I don't come inside. Remember last time?'

Leaving Luigi chuckling on the doorstep, she turned in the opposite direction to the one Greg had taken. Determined not to allow herself to be intimidated, she made for the nearest café, planning to continue her shopping once she had recovered her composure. But as she sipped a cup of strong coffee, her glance continually strayed to the lace-curtained window. Anyone passing only slightly resembling Greg caused her to tremble afresh.

As she watched, it suddenly occurred to her that Greg had known Marco had left Venice. How could he have known, unless he had observed Marco leaving that morning? Or perhaps Greg and Jonathan Webb were better acquainted than he was willing to admit, and it was Webb who had given him the information.

CHAPTER EIGHT

Troubled by her encounter with Greg, Kate returned home earlier than expected with the excuse of the weather being too unpredictable. She wondered about the letter he'd supposedly sent to Marco, or was it simply an empty threat, his way of manipulating her to gain entry to the palazzo?

She'd been distressed by the way her employment back home had been terminated, and although her employer had denied her a reason, she'd felt a cloud on her conscience, almost as if she had been accused outright of stealing. Her aunt had believed she was innocent, but what would Marco think if Greg had sent a letter suggesting she was guilty?

The following day, though determined not to allow the worry of Greg to keep her indoors, she experienced a curious sense of relief to see the weather was far from perfect as predicted. Greg always hated being out in the wind and rain, so it was unlikely she would encounter him today.

'I shouldn't go too far. By the look of the sky there's a storm brewing,' her aunt advised. 'According to the weather report, heavy rain and gales are forecast for the next few days.'

'That is exactly why I'm going, to see what all this talk of a storm is about. I've heard about the flooding, and Saint Mark's Square being under water. They say it's quite spectacular.'

Making sure Greg was nowhere in the vicinity, Kate strolled towards the Grand Canal, feeling the force of the wind on her face as she left the narrow street. There she saw boats buffeting noisily against their moorings as their owners strove to make them secure against the roughening waters.

This was a very different scene from the one she had come upon the day of her arrival and, to everyone's concern, the following day was the same. Only the sturdily-built waterbuses and motor launches ploughed their way through the turbulent waters of the Grand Canal and the wide lagoon.

Keeping well away from the narrow streets and the vicinity of Greg's hotel, Kate strolled along the waterside, watching the waves spray over the crowded moorings in Saint Mark's basin. She prayed the stormy outlook would keep Greg indoors. Then, furious with herself for allowing thought of him to intimidate her, she walked on until the rain increased to a steady downpour when she had to retrace her steps. As she hurried back to the house, thoughts of Marco's return lifted her spirits. Only two more days.

Smiling to herself, she jumped over the rapidly forming puddles on the uneven paving of the empty street until she was jerked back to the present by the harsh sound of an engine revving loudly from somewhere near the palazzo. She was just approaching the stone bridge when the echoing roar made her hurry forward in time to see a boat moving at high speed along the narrow canal. Though she couldn't tell who was at the helm, her heart lurched when she caught a glimpse of the emblem on its side. It was a large golden bird.

Filled with concern over the dangerous speed of the boat, she was about to turn in the direction of home when the sound of a terrified voice reached her ears. She paused. There it was again, a high-pitched scream, and another, muffled this time, coming from the direction of the canal. Heedless of the pouring rain, Kate moved quickly in the direction from where the sound came. Arriving at the bridge, she looked over the parapet. There was someone in the canal, clinging desperately to the iron bars of the gate safeguarding the entrance to Marco's boathouse.

With Marco away, she knew it would be a waste of time to call in at the palazzo for help so, seeing no-one close-by, she ran on to the bridge, casting aside her light waterproof coat. Without thought for her own safety, she pulled off her shoes and climbed over the lower end of the parapet to slide down into the swirling, dark water. Staying close to the damp, slimy wall of the palazzo as a safeguard against being struck by a boat, she swam strongly towards the gateway of the boathouse. As she drew near to the terrified form still clinging to the bars, she raised her head to assess the situation and gave a choking gasp of recognition.

With her long black hair moulded wetly to her head, Camilla bobbed up and down in the turbulent water, her screams of terror turning to sobs of relief as Kate came up beside her.

97

'Don't panic!' Kate directed firmly, grabbing for the iron grille where she attempted to recover her breath. 'Just hang on.'

But Camilla, wide-eyed with fear, let go of the bars and made a grab for Kate, almost pulling her under the water.

'Hold the bars,' Kate shouted, keeping Camilla's head above water with one arm, 'or you'll have us both drowned!'

Thankfully, Camilla obeyed, releasing the strain on Kate as she took further steadying breaths. Remembering the life-saving technique she had been taught during her schooldays, Kate took hold of Camilla and pushed herself away from the canal wall. With a sharp word of instruction, she kept the woman's head above water and swam the short distance to the bridge.

By the time they reached it, someone was calling from the parapet above and waving frantically at a launch that was coming in their direction. Wondering how she was going to get Camilla out of the water, she felt a surge of relief when the boat slackened speed and drew alongside.

It didn't take long for the owner of the water-taxi to haul the spluttering, sobbing Italian woman aboard with the offer to take her home. And, once she had satisfied herself Camilla was to be taken almost to her doorstep, Kate declined the boatman's offer of assistance, assuring him she was quite capable of climbing on to the bridge when she would be almost home.

Reaching for a finger-hold on the wall, she managed to haul herself from the water on to a narrow, stone ledge and glanced across to see the owner of the boat wrap a blanket around Camilla's shivering form. The woman appeared desperate to catch her attention so she held on.

'Don't tell Marco,' Camilla cried through chattering teeth, 'or Signora Rossini, please, Kathrine,' she implored. 'They must not know of this.'

Then her voice faded, drowned by the noise of the boat's engine. Kate almost slipped black into the water as the wake from the boat washed against her, but a man on the parapet called down. With aching muscles, she struggled to get her foot on to the next ledge when, with a grunt of extra effort, the man reached down a little farther and caught hold of her wrist. Once she could support her own weight, it was easy for him to grasp both her hands and help her over the parapet.

Reaching the safety of the bridge, she uttered a shuddering gasp and attempted to express her gratitude to the man who regarded her with puzzled interest. When she managed to explain why she had chosen to climb back on to the bridge rather than take the water-taxi, he appeared relieved, satisfied she would be home and dry in minutes. Draping her coat around her shoulders, he praised the English signorina for her bravery.

Suddenly, aware a number of people were beginning to collect around them, she realised her sodden appearance was causing more interest than she cared for. So, thanking the man once more, she slipped on her shoes and made off in the direction of her aunt's house. Recalling the woman's plea not to mention the incident, she climbed the stairs and made straight for the bathroom. However, before she reached it, her aunt spotted her.

'Good gracious!' she cried in horror. 'You look as though you've been in the canal!'

'I have,' Kate replied, striving to control her chattering teeth, 'and I'm about to run a hot bath and get out of these wet things. I'll explain later.'

'I should have warned you. The paving can be extremely slippery just now. You must be more careful,' the signora fussed as Kate disappeared into the bathroom.

Lying in the hot, scented water, Kate thought again about how Camilla had begged her not to mention the incident to her aunt or Marco. Why make such a request, she wondered, and how had she come to be in the water in the first place? Reflecting on the unglamorous picture Camilla presented as she struggled in the water, Kate knew for certain she could only have got there by accident. Yet, being familiar with her surroundings, it was unlikely she had slipped into the canal dressed in some fashionable creation, particularly as she couldn't swim. Kate was convinced there was something very strange about the incident, and this disturbed her.

Cosily dressed in a tracksuit, she took the cup of steaming hot chocolate Rosa had prepared and sipped it gratefully. Only then did she realise she would be expected to account for her soaking but, after Camilla had begged her not to reveal the truth, how was she to explain?

'Now you can tell me what happened,' her aunt began as she refilled her cup. 'I could hardly believe my eyes when you came in. Thank goodness you're a strong swimmer, but it must have been difficult to get out.'

Kate searched her mind for an explanation.

'A man saw me from the bridge,' she began, 'and he helped me out. You see, someone had fallen in the water. I couldn't ignore her.'

'You mean, you've saved someone's life?' the signora exclaimed, sitting bolt upright in her chair. 'Was it a child? Where is she now?'

'Don't worry, she's quite safe,' Kate assured her, and rushed on evasively. 'I expect it's an everyday occurrence here—slippery paving, a careless step. I often fell in the river at home when I was a child.'

The signora's eyes narrowed.

'Kate, I suspect you are hiding something.'

she pressed. 'Who was it?'

Kate sighed and looked away.

'Actually, it was Camilla,' she admitted quietly, 'but please don't say anything as she didn't want you or Marco to know.'

The signora gasped and leaned towards her.

'Camilla!' she exclaimed, but Kate merely shook her head. 'But why ask you not to say anything? What could be her reason?'

'I haven't the faintest idea,' she said and went on to relate what had happened in the canal. 'Of course, by telling you, I've betrayed her trust,' she ended with a sigh, 'but promise me you won't say anything to Marco.'

'If that is what you wish,' she agreed, 'but I hardly think she had the right to ask. After all, you probably saved her life.'

'Oh, I'm sure the boat that came along would have picked her up, but what puzzles me is how she came to be there in the first place.'

'Yes, it's very strange. Was her launch anywhere near? Could she have fallen from it?'

'No, but just before I spotted Camilla, a boat went away under the bridge at a terrific speed, and if the emblem on hers is a gold bird, then I'm sure this one had the same thing on its side.'

'Did you see who was at the helm? I never did trust that man of hers.'

'Actually, I believe I saw two people, men, I

think, both wearing wetsuits, but I didn't recognise either of them.'

'Two? I wonder, could one have been Georgio?'

The signora thought for a moment then discarded the idea.

'No, I don't suppose he owns a wetsuit.'

Kate shook her head.

'I really couldn't say, but in any case it would have been most unlikely he'd have left Camilla in the water.'

'You're right, he's too much of a gentleman. Perhaps Marco can enlighten us.'

'Only if he brings the matter up,' Kate put in firmly, 'otherwise, I won't mention it. After all, it really isn't any concern of ours. As it's not a matter of life or death, I'll keep it to myself.'

'It almost was, both for Camilla and for you!' the signora countered crossly just as the telephone rang.

'It's for you, Kate,' she announced moments later.

'It's not Greg, is it?'

The signora shook her head and put her hand over the mouthpiece.

'No, but speak of the devil, it's Camilla!'

Kate experienced a twinge of apprehension as she took the receiver.

'Are you all right, Camilla?' she enquired and couldn't fail to hear the heartrending sobs that came over the line.

'You won't tell Marco, will you?' Camilla gasped.

'If that is what you want,' Kate agreed, 'but I'm afraid Signora Rossini had to know as I could hardly expect her not to notice my appearance.'

'Please, I beg you, ask her not to tell Marco.'

Kate's responding sigh of impatience was quickly cut short when Camilla continued, 'Greg Courtney—he makes trouble for you?'

'Greg! What has he got to do with it?' Kate demanded.

'He seeks revenge,' Camilla replied. 'He makes trouble for you. I warn you because you saved my life.'

'Otherwise, you wouldn't have bothered,' Kate put in icily, and when Camilla protested she cut her short. 'Don't you worry. Greg Courtney doesn't frighten me!'

She then replaced the receiver.

'What was all that about?' her aunt asked when Kate returned to her seat. 'You sounded extremely agitated.'

'I was! That stupid woman has been listening to Greg and his ridiculous threats, but I won't allow myself to be intimidated!'

'Do you suppose there's any truth in it? I mean, if he's likely to cause you trouble, I'll call the police.'

'No, I'm ignoring the whole thing,' she responded firmly. 'Whatever he threatens, I'm not lying about the accident merely to save his skin!'

After her exhausting experience in the canal, Kate decided to follow her aunt's example and take a short rest before tea. She was lying on the bed with her book opened at the page where she'd left it the previous day when there was a tap on the door of her room and Rosa peeped in.

'I am very worried,' Rosa began, 'and I don't want to disturb the signora as she is sleeping now.'

Kate beckoned Rosa into the room. The girl pointed towards the window.

'You can hear something, signorina? I believe someone is calling from near the palazzo. I think someone is ill.'

'Oh, no, not again!' Kate groaned.

Even so, she rose immediately and went to the window, straining her ears for a sound. Then, there it was, the weak cry of what sounded like a male voice but she couldn't distinguish what the words were. Struggling into thin cotton trousers and a T-shirt, she called Rosa over.

'Will you come with me? I can't tell where the voice is coming from, nor can I understand what he's saying.'

Outside, on the bridge, Kate paused, straining her ears as she tried to decide where the distressed cries came from. Rosa had gone ahead to the door of the palazzo garden, but soon signalled to say it was locked.

'I think it is coming from where the boat must go,' Rosa said, pointing in the direction of the heavy grille at the entrance to the boathouse. 'It's calling for help in Italian. Maybe it is Georgio.'

'I think he's away,' she said, but thought it worthwhile to call his name to which there came a wavering response.

'Si, si, it is Georgio,' Rosa confirmed excitedly.

'Ask him where he is, what is wrong, and can we get in?' Kate instructed, and heard Rosa convey her request in the man's own language.

'We must go to the main entrance,' Rosa translated after a few minutes' wait. 'This door is unlocked, and he is falling on the floor.'

'But how do we get to the entrance from here, Rosa?'

'A boat! We must have a boat. This door is flooded.'

Kate grabbed her hand.

'Come on,' she said briskly. 'We can get a water-taxi round the corner, but I'm afraid you'll have to speak for me and explain that we'll pay later.'

At first they had a negative response from the boat owner until Rosa explained the reason for their short journey. Then, albeit reluctantly, he helped them into his craft and soon they were on the Grand Canal, mooring as close as it was possible to the palazzo's main entrance.

'Rosa, ask him to wait,' Kate directed, splashing over the flooded steps to reach the heavy main door.

With Rosa beside her, they made their way into the building, arriving in the cool courtyard where she called Georgio's name again. Recalling the direction of the passage leading to the boathouse, she hurried along as Georgia's voice grew clearer. And there, halfway down the flight of steps, they found him, struggling to drag himself up.

'There you are,' Kate said gently, her professional manner coming to the fore. 'Now don't worry, we'll soon have you more comfortable,' she continued, observing the man's shocked state. 'Translate for me, will you, Rosa? And do stay calm. I'm just going to check him over before he moves any farther. The position of his right leg doesn't look too good to me.'

Kate made a brief examination of the state of Georgio's health. The wound on his head was still oozing blood, and by what she could detect, he had been rendered unconscious by his fall. The position of his leg really worried her. Only a broken limb could lie in such a twisted way.

'He has just returned from Padua,' Rosa translated, 'and he was concerned about the boathouse in the flood.'

'I see,' Kate broke in. 'Well, he requires

hospital treatment so will you go back and ask my aunt if she knows the name of Georgio's doctor? Tell her we require an ambulance. Also, ask her for money to pay the boatman.'

CHAPTER NINE

Kate stifled a sigh of relief when the doctor arrived. She had covered Georgio's shaking form with the blankets Rosa had found, and with one of her aunt's clean towels against the wound on his head and a cushion tucked beneath it, she had managed to make him more comfortable.

As the doctor slid a needle into a vein in Georgio's arm he praised her efforts to keep his patient in a stable condition until the extent of his injuries became known. Rosa had been asked to await the medical team and bring them into the building, and it wasn't too long before they arrived to manoeuvre Georgio on to the special stretcher and carry him off to the ambulance boat.

'I think I'd better take charge of the keys after we've locked up,' Kate said. 'Signora Rossini will know what to do.'

Thankfully, their boatman was still waiting when they went out by the main entrance and locked the door. He took them back into the narrow canal where they struggled to disembark on the flooded sidewalk. Rosa paid him the required amount.

'One way or another, it's been quite a day!' she said once safely back in her aunt's house. 'Thank goodness Rosa heard poor Georgio.'

'Rosa believes he must have fallen on the steps but she couldn't quite make out what he was saying. I'll telephone the hospital later to enquire.'

'Marco will get a shock when he returns to find Georgio in hospital,' Kate remarked. 'And if he knew about the Camilla incident as well, I can't imagine what he would say.'

'If it hadn't been for you and Rosa, they both could be dead by now.'

'Oh, I doubt that, somebody would have heard them,' Kate responded with a modest shrug, 'although I must confess, I quite enjoyed putting my nursing skills into practice again.'

'Yes, Marco was most relieved to know you had rendered first aid.'

'You mean you've spoken to him?' Kate queried. 'When was that?'

'I have the number of his mobile phone, so I thought it only right to let him know Georgio is in safe hands.'

Later that afternoon, Kate received a phone call and the signora was delighted when Kate related the message.

'It was Marco,' Kate announced happily. 'He's coming back earlier than he originally intended and wants to take me out to dinner after he has visited the hospital this evening.'

'Oh, I'm so pleased for you, dear,' Aunt Margaret said happily. 'I'm sure everything will be all right between you now.'

'Perhaps his impression of me is not as bad as I'd imagined,' she said with optimistic cheerfulness, 'though he did say there were things we should discuss.'

'Then let us hope it is not in connection with what happened in the canal this afternoon. I'm worried, Kate. That devious creature is up to something, I'm sure, and I don't like it.'

'If you mean Camilla,' Kate replied, 'she's the least of my worries.'

But even as she brushed aside her aunt's concern, deep down, the reason Camilla had warned her about Greg continued to bother her. She wondered if Camilla had been in conversation with him and, if so, what had they discussed. Even more important, had Greg carried out his threat to reveal to Marco the reason Kate was no longer employed?

However, when Marco called later that day to announce his return, all her worries over Camilla and Greg were completely dispelled.

'Can you be ready in fifteen minutes, Kathrine?' he asked, and she had difficulty keeping the note of eagerness from her voice when she agreed.

'I have visited the hospital and had a word

with the doctor,' he continued. 'Evidently Georgio has suffered a compound fracture, also a great deal of bruising to his ribs. However, I was unable to speak with him as he was still under the anaesthetic.'

'I suspected it was a bad break when I discovered him, though he's in the best place possible,' she ended comfortingly.

'Thanks to you,' he said, and she could detect a smile in his voice. 'I shall telephone the hospital later, meanwhile I will hire a boat to take us to our little waterside café.'

'I shall look forward to that,' she murmured, replacing the receiver.

When the doorbell rang a short time later, she didn't use the intercom or wait for Rosa, but went down to open the door to Marco herself.

'How long have you been back?' she asked as he took her hand to lead her in the direction of the canal.

'Only seconds before I last spoke with you,' he replied with a smile. 'I haven't yet checked for business messages, or looked around the place. I just showered and changed, and hurried over here to take you to dinner.'

'I'm flattered,' she murmured.

'I asked for a table in a secluded corner so that we can talk in peace,' he told her, squeezing her hand. 'And by not taking my own boat, no-one will know we are there.'

It didn't take long for the hired water-taxi to

find its way to the little café. She noticed the proprietor glancing expectantly from the doorway, and on seeing them disembark he rushed over the paving to greet them. With a huge smile, he led them to the far end of the long room where he drew back a beaded curtain to reveal a cosy alcove. The table was covered in spotless white linen and in the centre stood a slim vase holding a single red rose.

'Now I have you to myself,' Marco began as the proprietor withdrew with their order. 'Tell me what has been happening during my absence.'

'Well, you know about Georgio's accident,' she managed to respond, concealing the matter of Camilla. 'Otherwise, little else happened worth mentioning. How about you? Was your business trip successful?'

'I think so,' he said slowly. 'I now have Camilla's financial affairs in order and no further responsibility in that direction. In addition, I have acquired three beautiful paintings of Carlo's for which Camilla had little regard. They will make a perfect display at the exhibition.'

'Camilla?' she queried with a slight frown. 'Considering she is arranging your exhibition, I assumed she would appreciate art.'

Marco leaned forward, brows raised.

'I regret to say Camilla doesn't appreciate Carlo's work, only enjoys the fame and attention which goes with it. But I want to see you smile again so let us forget everything else. We are here to celebrate. To begin, we should celebrate just being together, and then, well, who knows?'

Just then, the proprietor brushed through the curtain to place an ice bucket beside their table, and once he had the bottle of champagne expertly uncorked, he filled the two tall glasses.

'To us,' Marco said, raising his glass as he went on to add, 'I have missed you so, Kathrine,' and before she could respond he continued, 'During the time I was away you were constantly in my thoughts.'

'Was I really?' she murmured, happiness rising within her.

'Yes, constantly. Did you miss me?'

'Yes, I did,' she began, pausing as their first course arrived and she plunged into a more familiar topic. 'Of course, it's been raining hard most of the time, and we've had extremely strong winds.'

'Which is another reason I came back earlier than intended. I didn't want to find the whole place awash, and I must inspect the door leading to the boathouse. Although it doesn't hold back the water during a very strong tide, it does keep out the rubbish.'

At once, her thoughts flew back to her experience in the canal that afternoon and she shuddered.

'But I haven't brought you here to discuss flooding, Kathrine. I wish to know more about you.'

'I think you already know most things,' she said a trifle uneasily. 'I'm just a very ordinary person.'

'Hardly,' he said with a smile. 'I've seen you grow from a very pretty schoolgirl into a beautiful young woman who is far from ordinary.'

Her eyes widened, then she smiled as she realised what he meant.

'You're referring to the photographs my aunt keeps in her album.'

'Signora Rossini is always so proud of you. She often showed them to me, and I do believe I was a little in love with you then,' he ended reflectively as he took up his glass.

'Merely a schoolboy crush, I'm sure,' she supplied with a nervous laugh.

'My dear Kathrine, I most certainly was not a schoolboy. Had you not realised, I am at least ten years older than you?'

'Now you're teasing,' she said. 'No-one falls in love with a photograph.'

'Maybe I didn't realise it at the time, but during the last few days I have become extremely aware of what has been tormenting me. You see, Kathrine, I feel I have known you for longer than the short time you have been in Venice, and long enough for me to want to know your feelings.'

'My feelings, Marco?' she queried hesitantly. 'Do you mean . . .'

'Yes, your feelings for me,' he replied, taking her hand once more.

For a moment she was silent. She wanted to blurt out just how much she loved him, tell him he meant everything to her, but something held her back.

'I like you very much,' she whispered.

'Enough to marry me?' he asked softly as his fingers entwined with hers.

'Marry you!' she exclaimed in a hushed voiced. 'Are you serious?'

'Never more so. This was my reason for a celebration.'

'But you hardly know me,' she began breathlessly.

'Quite long enough to know you are kind and gentle, and sincere. You made me aware of that when I was a little overbearing with you once before. Now I find you possess many other qualities.'

Kate swallowed hard. Sincere! Marco didn't know everything. She couldn't possibly give him an answer, not now, with Greg and the problem of the summons hanging over her, in addition to the mystery concerning Camilla. What reply could she possibly give?

Kate spent a very restless night. Of course she wanted to be Marco's wife, more than anything else, but she couldn't possibly accept. She'd agreed that she could very happily live in

Venice, but still couldn't bring herself to reply to his proposal. He hadn't pressed her further, offering her a little more time to think it over.

'I assume your evening didn't turn out as well as you expected,' Signora Rossini commented the following day when she saw Kate's rather troubled expression. 'I thought you and Marco were good friends once more.'

'Oh, yes, we are,' Kate replied. 'In fact, he proposed to me last night.'

'Oh, my dear, I'm so pleased for you. I suspected he was in love with you, remember? You do love Marco?'

'You know I do,' Kate replied, 'but I can't agree to marry him until I've got the problem of Greg and that summons off my mind. Also, there's something nagging me regarding Camilla and her warning about Greg, and insisting Marco shouldn't know other escapade in the canal.'

'Darling, do remember you are not at fault in any way, and whatever Greg or Camilla choose to do is no concern of yours. Let them solve their own problems,' the signora advised kindly, 'and put them out of your mind.'

'Thanks,' Kate said warmly, 'I needed that pep talk. Somehow, Greg has made me feel like a criminal and I just wish he would own up.'

'Why not deal with that matter when, or if, it arises,' the signora suggested wisely. 'Personally, I think he's bluffing, though I'm sure Marco can advise you. After all, he has studied law.'

'I promised to ring Marco this morning, but before I agree to marry him I've decided to tell him the truth. I don't want to hide anything from him.'

'An ideal way to start a marriage,' the signora said approvingly. 'But what about the Camilla incident. Doesn't that count?'

'Yes, I suppose you're right,' Kate agreed thoughtfully then, recalling something Marco had said the previous evening, asked, 'By the way, do you know the connection between Camilla and the paintings?'

'Well, Camilla hurt Marco terribly. You see, she likes to live her life as though there's no tomorrow, and to repay her debts she sold some valuable paintings of Carlo's which originally had been intended for Marco. I believe she sold them to raise money for her trips around Europe.'

'Last night Marco said he had acquired three paintings during the time he was away,' Kate put in. 'He appeared highly delighted about it.'

'Oh, that is good news!' the signora exclaimed joyfully. 'I expect it is part of the collection I've just mentioned.'

'I gather from what he said, Camilla doesn't appreciate art so I suppose she wouldn't mind parting with them.'

'You suppose correctly. Marco must have

contacted every art dealer in the country in an effort to get them back. Now, don't you think it is time you rang Marco to enquire after Georgio's progress?'

Kate got her feet just as the telephone rang. The signora indicated for Kate to answer it.

'I was just about to ring you to ask about Georgio, I expect he will be conscious by now,' Kate began happily the moment she heard Marco's voice. 'And there's something I would like to discuss with you, assuming it is convenient for me to come over this morning.'

'So, you have something to confess?' he responded shortly, his tone bitter, making her wonder what he already knew.

'I don't want there to be any misunderstanding between us.'

'Misunderstanding!' he exclaimed. 'I consider that an understatement.'

'I'll come over,' she said hurriedly, and, replacing the receiver, turned an anxious face to her aunt to ask, 'You haven't said anything about the summons, have you?'

'Of course not, dear. Why do you ask?'

'Marco sounded very annoyed. I'd better get over there right away.'

CHAPTER TEN

It was Marco himself who called her in, and she hesitated as she saw him standing at the top of the wide staircase, his expression grim. He gave a curt gesture for her to join him.

'Come into the study,' he directed coolly, marching ahead.

When she reached it, he was standing with his back to the window.

'Is something wrong?' she asked, rushing on to add, 'If it's anything to do with Greg Courtney and the accident, I can explain. In fact, that is what I want to speak to you about.'

He raised his brows and queried, 'Accident?' as he went to seat himself behind his desk and beckoned her to the chair opposite. 'Yes, tell me about this accident.'

She was a little uncertain of where to begin.

'Do you recall the occasion when I was mistakenly thought to have been in Greg Courtney's hotel room?' she began at last.

'Mistakenly or not, I do,' he replied.

'I was there only a few minutes,' she insisted, 'just long enough to read a letter from his solicitor regarding a forthcoming summons.'

Noting a sudden spark of interest in his expression, she hesitated. Obviously, this was something he hadn't expected. Frowning, he gestured for her to go on.

'Perhaps I should explain how the accident happened,' she offered, and plunged into the full story, including details of her own injuries and the fact Greg had put the blame on her, saying she was driving when making his original statement. 'And now he expects me to continue to lie for him,' she ended with a despondent sigh.

Marco sat back in his chair, his expression thoughtful as he warned, 'It would amount to perjury, Kathrine.'

'I know, which is why I will not do it, whatever he threatens.'

He nodded, but when he remained silent she went on.

'I couldn't give an answer to your marriage proposal, not with this hanging over me, at least, not until I'd spoken to you about it.'

Her voice trailed off when Marco made no response. But she continued.

'Does it make such a difference? I mean, I have explained, so I hope you don't think I'm at fault.'

He gave a mirthless laugh and rose to his feet.

'My dear Kathrine!' he exclaimed with an expressive lift of his shoulders. 'What you have just told me has no connection with my problem here! Somehow, I have become a victim of my own foolishness,' he declared, his tone bitter. 'Come with me and observe the result.'

Curious as to what could possibly be wrong, she hurried behind Marco along the corridor leading towards the room containing his valuable works of art. Whatever it was, it had disturbed him deeply, and it seemed he thought her to be somehow involved. At the door of the room, he paused.

'This is what I returned home to find,' he told her grimly as he pushed it open. 'I wonder if you can also explain this!'

For a second Kate couldn't understand his anger until she moved farther into the room and saw the wall which had once been filled with beautiful works of art. Now there were two empty spaces on the lower row, and three more on the one above. Five of Marco's most valued pictures had disappeared, their empty frames cast aside on the floor below.

'Your pictures!' she gasped and turned to meet his hard stare. 'But surely you don't think I had anything to do with it?'

He gestured towards the ornate table in the corner upon which, to her amazement, she saw the little crocheted bag Rosa had made for her.

'Yours, I believe?' he said, extending his arm to prevent her retrieving it.

'Yes, but I didn't leave it in here,' she cried. 'It was either in the cloakroom, or the sitting-room. I didn't miss it until after you left.'

She looked up to find Marco's expression

had softened a little.

'I rather thought you hadn't,' he said more gently. 'It is too obvious. But someone placed it there to incriminate you, so don't touch anything.'

'But who would want to incriminate me?'

'That is exactly what I intend to find out!' he told her, but before he could continue, his housekeeper appeared in the doorway to call his attention.

Feeling utterly distraught, Kate gazed in dismay on the pile of empty frames as she waited for Marco to return. Then, suddenly, a dreadful thought occurred to her and her heart sank. Could this be Greg's way of taking his revenge? He knew Marco was away, but how could he have entered the palazzo?

When Marco came back she looked up to meet his steely gaze when he demanded, 'Why didn't you tell me you met Courtney whilst I was away?'

'I didn't meet him,' she denied furiously. 'He happened to be on the same street!'

'So, it was him,' he said with a bitter smile. 'Luigi described our, er, robber, perfectly. It was only by chance my housekeeper met Luigi this morning and, thank God, she is of a curious nature, otherwise I should not have known.'

'There is nothing to know!' she cried. 'I hardly spoke to Greg.'

'But he threatened you. Luigi heard him,

and you were very upset,' he stated, reaching for her. 'Did he persuade you to let him into the palazzo and tell him where my pictures are kept? After all, I believe you are in possession of Georgio's keys.'

'No, Marco, no,' she denied wildly. 'I wouldn't have told him that! In any case, my aunt has the keys!'

Retaining his hold on her, Marco continued, 'So, if he didn't coerce you into helping him, why were you so nervous? Kathrine, you must tell me all you know before I call in the police.'

'He wanted an introduction to the palazzo, but I didn't allow him to intimidate me. How could you even think I would!' she cried. 'But I can't prove my innocence. You'll have to accept my word.'

He uttered a harsh sigh and spread his hands in a helpless gesture.

'I do, but I wish you had been frank with me before I left,' he said heavily. 'Now you are threatened, my paintings stolen, and there's a connection somewhere, I'm certain.'

Deeply hurt, Kate couldn't help but feel he was accusing her of being involved, and she spun away from him.

'I don't know anything about your damned paintings!' she cried as she sped towards the staircase. 'Just leave me out of it!'

'Kathrine, come back!' she heard as she ran down the steps. 'Please, Kathrine, come back!' he repeated, but she rushed on heedless.

123

By the time she reached the door to her aunt's home, her anger was beginning to subside and uncertainty was creeping in. Was Marco accusing her of assisting the thief, or was his only concern that someone was trying to place the blame on her? She was certain that that someone was Greg. Hadn't Camilla warned her, and who else would wish to incriminate her?

Confident Greg was the culprit she decided to confront him right away, and it was as she hurried in the direction of his hotel that another thought struck her. Was Greg the only one to blame, or had Camilla assisted him? Also, what reason was there for Camilla being in the canal? Was there a connection between that incident and the missing paintings?

At the hotel reception she asked to see Greg but was dismayed to learn he had checked out earlier in the day. Her spirit of determination began to ebb as she left the building to walk disconsolately along the narrow street. But she had barely gone more than a few yards when she heard her name and glanced back to see Marco about to enter the hotel, accompanied by two men in uniform.

'Kathrine!' he called sharply. 'What on earth are you doing here?'

'Merely hoping to prove my innocence,' she returned, adding sarcastically, 'though I expect you assumed I'd come to warn him!'

'Don't be ridiculous!' he snapped. 'You are

not under suspicion.'

'I'd begun to doubt that!' she retaliated. 'But we've both made a wasted journey. He's already left!'

She heard Marco's muffled curse, then he hailed her once more.

'I'll see you later. I want to know how the devil you and Camilla came to be in the canal!'

'Why don't you ask her?' Kate shot back and saw the policemen direct him towards the water's edge.

'I intend to!' he returned before moving quickly out of sight in the direction of the waiting launch.

There was now nothing left to do but go home, she decided dismally as she retraced her steps. Yet, when she reached the house she found her aunt in a very agitated state.

'Where on earth have you been?' the signora demanded crossly. 'Marco telephoned more than half an hour ago, expecting you to be here.'

'So much has happened today, you would never believe it!'

'Yes, I would,' her aunt replied. 'Marco told me all about it when he rang. Now he's gone off to find Courtney so, hopefully, it will all be sorted out.'

'I know, I've just seen him, but I'm afraid we were both unlucky. Greg's already checked out of his hotel.'

'You went to his hotel? Oh, Kate, that

wasn't very wise!'

'I wanted to challenge him about the theft, but I was too late,' she explained, and on a sudden thought asked, 'By the way, how did Marco find out I'd been in the canal?'

'I told him,' the signora admitted defiantly. 'As soon as he told me they had discovered entry to the palazzo had been gained by way of the boathouse, I was convinced that Camilla had something to do with it. I'm sorry to break a confidence, but I felt he ought to know.'

With a sad shake of her head, Kate agreed.

'It really doesn't matter any more. I'm tired of hearing about Camilla, and paintings, also the fact I seem to be involved. It's just too much!'

Signora Rossini's brows lifted in surprise.

'Really, Kate,' she said gently, 'this is not like you. Marco doesn't consider you are at fault, you know. He's more concerned with who has tried to involve you, and he was horrified when he heard about you risking your life in the canal.'

'I would hardly have described him as horrified or concerned this morning!' Kate exclaimed indignantly.

'Yes, he admitted he had upset you. He will want to make amends.'

'I'd rather he didn't bother,' Kate began. 'He's so arrogant! I hate him!'

'He believes passionately in fair play, but arrogant, certainly not!' the signora admonished. 'He'll stand by you, my dear, because he loves you.'

*   *   *

It was in the early evening when Marco called. Kate wasn't prepared for his visit and quickly rose from the settee, seeking an excuse to escape.

'Please stay, Kathrine, I have a great deal to tell you,' he insisted.

'I'm not in the least interested in anything you have to say,' she responded bitterly, turning away.

'But before I continue,' he persisted, 'I want you to believe I hold you in no way responsible for what has happened.'

'That wasn't the impression I had earlier!' she shot back angrily. 'In fact, I almost expected to be arrested by those policemen you had with you!'

'Obviously, I must have expressed myself badly and I hope you will forgive me if I gave that impression.'

'It really doesn't matter, one way or the other,' she shrugged.

'Oh, yes, it does!' he declared passionately, advancing towards her. 'Before you condemn me, you will listen to what I have to say.'

'No, Marco,' she retorted. 'There's nothing more to say.'

'Kathrine, I have asked you to be my wife,'

127

he reminded her more gently. 'Doesn't that give an indication of my true feelings towards you?'

The appeal in his eyes began to melt her anger, and with a long, wavering sigh she shook her head and said brokenly, 'I'm so confused, I don't know what to believe.'

'Believe me, Kathrine,' he murmured. 'I'll always love and protect you.'

'Oh, Marco, I want to, but with this hanging over me how can I . . .'

She spread her hands in a helpless gesture as the signora came into the room. Marco indicated for her to stay, and, placing an arm round Kate's shoulders, he led her over to the settee.

'I have made a great deal of progress since I last spoke with you,' he said, seating himself beside her. 'After you saw me at the hotel I went immediately to the airport.'

'Why the airport?'

'Because that was where I hoped to find Courtney, and I was right. He was waiting for his flight back to London.'

'You saw him!' she cried. 'What did he say?'

Marco looked at her with laughter in his eyes.

'Kathrine, if you continue to interrupt I shall use devious means to silence you,' he threatened, then went on to say, 'I wish you could have seen his expression when the police arrested him. He was absolutely astounded!

And, can you believe it, he actually had the paintings with him, simply rolled up in a plastic bag!'

'But you got them back?' she asked anxiously.

'Yes, I did, though at first he wouldn't admit to taking them. He told me Camilla had given them to him, and he had presumed they belonged to her.'

'Can they be restored?'

'I expect so as they were removed with reasonable care though, unfortunately, it will delay the exhibition,' he told her. 'However, here comes the interesting part. Guess who was travelling with him?'

'Who? Please, Marco, don't keep me in suspense.'

'Our American friend, Webb, who soon lost his accent in the scuffle. Of course, Webb denied knowing Courtney. He got quite nasty. But when more police arrived he soon backed down. According to the police,' he went on, 'Webb has been involved in art theft all over Europe, and used Greg in the process, and now I understand they were responsible for a theft from your previous employer.'

Kate's eyes narrowed.

'How did you know about that?' she asked, with a glance in her aunt's direction.

'You were going to tell him about that yourself,' the signora reminded her, 'so there was no point in delaying.'

Marco smiled.

'You have no need to worry, Kathrine. I didn't consider you at fault. After you rushed away from me earlier, Signora Rossini and I had a little chat, and it was then I learned about the dreadful time you have had concerning the accident and your loss of employment. You have suffered all this unnecessarily as, if I had known before, I could have advised you about what steps to take.'

'I realise that now. I was sure I'd met Webb before, and when both he and Courtney turned up here it seemed more than just a coincidence.'

'Indeed it was, and they both tried to implicate you in the theft. Of course, I realised Webb was a professional thief and Courtney merely a weak character who was easily manipulated. This being so, Courtney quickly confessed to how the theft had been committed.'

'Did you discover what part Camilla played in all this?' Signora Rossini queried with a shrewd glance in her niece's direction.

'Indeed, I did,' he said gravely. 'I left a very subdued Camilla after we had spoken about the trouble she has caused, and this time she had the decency to appear contrite. She tells me she was on the point of coming to me with her confession. After what you did, Kathrine, she actually felt guilty. Knowing you would risk your life for her after she had helped Webb and Courtney with their plans to discredit you made her realise what a fool she had been. But in future she must take responsibility for her own recklessness. I've done everything Carlo expected of me so I suggested she leave Venice.'

He broke off and turned to Kate, taking her hand as he went on.

'Actually, I found her only too willing to comply.'

'What puzzles me is, how did Camilla come to be in the water in the first place?' Kate said.

'It seems that Courtney and Webb used her launch and she had acted as lookout for when they came out with the goods. But in their hurry to get away she fell into the water.'

'Fortunately for Camilla, Kate spotted her shortly afterwards,' the signora put in.

'She tells me it was all Courtney's and Webb's doing,' Marco said. 'Evidently they wore wet suits to enter the palazzo by swimming under the boathouse grille and breaking the bolt on the inner door while she waited in her launch. According to her, Webb took over the wheel and pulled away so quickly she fell overboard.'

'Her launch?' Kate queried, recalling how she'd caught a glimpse of a boat speeding away just before she had heard Camilla's cries for help.

'Yes, her boat,' Marco confirmed, 'and not the first time she has caused trouble with it.

Remember, near our little restaurant? However, on this occasion, Webb and Courtney contrived to use her launch purely for their own convenience. Georgio was fully conscious when the police and I visited this afternoon and he told us he'd found the inner boathouse door was damaged and blamed the pressure of the floodwater, until he was knocked down the steps by the escaping thieves. Of course, when I returned nothing appeared to have been disturbed, that is, until this morning when I unlocked the room where my paintings are kept.'

'And you immediately thought I was the culprit,' she reminded him.

'Of course not!' he exclaimed with a sigh of exasperation. 'But I was concerned Courtney might have pressed you into telling him where the paintings were, though I know you wouldn't have been a willing partner.'

'I suppose I should at least be grateful for that!' she rejoined.

'Ah, yes, but do remember, you had shown an interest in who would be left in charge of the palazzo whilst I was away. You knew where I kept the key and, as you are now aware, Courtney had been overheard threatening you. Oh, Kathrine, you must understand, I was so furious it rocked my judgment, and if I gave the wrong impression I'm extremely sorry.'

Meeting the appeal in his eyes, Kate couldn't help but smile and, taking this as a

132

sign of forgiveness, Marco cupped her face in his warm hands and kissed her. A little surprised by this show of affection, she drew away and glanced towards the chair opposite, but the signora was no longer there. Marco chuckled.

'Yes, we are alone, and now the time has come for you to give me your answer,' he said softly as he drew her close. 'I love you so much and, more than anything, I want you to be my wife.'

'So you do trust me?' she whispered, looking up into his eyes.

'Completely, darling,' he murmured against her cheek, 'and I will never allow anyone to come between us,' he continued before capturing her lips once more.

'I must go home next week,' she reminded him as they drew apart. 'My ticket expires, and my parents, they ought to know everything.'

He raised a dark brow.

'Know? Does that mean your answer is "yes"?'

'Yes, Marco,' she replied on a deep sigh, 'but I'd like to return and be married in Venice.'

'Then I shall accompany you back home,' he declared. 'I cannot bear being parted from you ever again.'

133

We hope you have enjoyed this Large Print book. Other Chivers Press or Thorndike Press Large Print books are available at your library or directly from the publishers.

For more information about current and forthcoming titles, please call or write, without obligation, to:

Chivers Large Print
published by BBC Audiobooks Ltd
St James House, The Square
Lower Bristol Road
Bath BA2 3BH
UK
email: bbcaudiobooks@bbc.co.uk
www.bbcaudiobooks.co.uk

OR

Thorndike Press
295 Kennedy Memorial Drive
Waterville
Maine 04901
USA
www.gale.com/thorndike
www.gale.com/wheeler

All our Large Print titles are designed for easy reading, and all our books are made to last.